"You've got to help me," Ben whispered

Mel shut the oven door and turned around to see a desperate expression on her handsome boss's face.

"Miss Gorgeous not falling for your charm?" Mel was sure most women did. She reminded herself not to. She knew too much about marriage-shy men.

"Contrary to what you believe, I do not sleep with every woman that bats her eyelashes at me." He stopped, as if thinking. "At least, not until now. I get the feeling the minute I get her clothes off, she's going to slap a marriage certificate on the pillow."

Mel picked up a spoon and stirred her gravy. "Poor man. You have a beautiful ex-Miss Texas at your house for the weekend. What do you expect me to do about it?"

"Poison her?"

Mel gave him a withering look. "I've only worked for you for two days and you're asking me to commit murder?" She started to chuckle. He was an outrageous man, but he made her laugh.

He smiled a completely charming smile and stepped a little too close to her for comfort. "We're in this together. Your job is to protect me. One wrong step and I'll be walking down the aisle...."

Dear Reader,

Several years ago I sat in my living room and watched as Oprah introduced a roomful of "Alaska Men" to the single women of Chicago. This was the first time the concept of "Mail Order Men" had been brought to national television and, I admit, the mind of a happily married romance writer whirled with all of the exciting possibilities. I confess to videotaping the show and watching it more than once. I imagined more happy endings than Oprah could list, and I've often wondered what happened to those strangers coupled together for a night on the town. Did they live happily ever after, snuggled under down quilts during long, Alaskan winters? I hope so.

I waited a long time to write a story like this. My own "mail order man," Texas rancher Ben Bradley, is about to meet the three women who have answered his ad in *Texas Men,* a magazine full of eligible bachelors just dying to meet the right woman. Only, Ben didn't place the ad, didn't even know the darn thing existed, and of all the women who appear on the doorstep of the Triple Bar S, only one will win his heart. Mel Madison is the least likely candidate for romance, of course. She's shy and plain and…pregnant, not the kind of woman who is the least bit interested in falling in love with a hell-raising cowboy.

I thought she and Ben would be perfect together. And I hope you will, too!

All my best,

Kristine Rolofson

Kristine Rolofson
THE TEXAN TAKES A WIFE

Harlequin Books

TORONTO • NEW YORK • LONDON
AMSTERDAM • PARIS • SYDNEY • HAMBURG
STOCKHOLM • ATHENS • TOKYO • MILAN
MADRID • WARSAW • BUDAPEST • AUCKLAND

If you purchased this book without a cover you should be aware that this book is stolen property. It was reported as "unsold and destroyed" to the publisher, and neither the author nor the publisher has received any payment for this "stripped book."

To Glen, who makes it all possible

ISBN 0-373-25704-X

THE TEXAN TAKES A WIFE

Copyright © 1996 by Kristine Rolofson.

All rights reserved. Except for use in any review, the reproduction or utilization of this work in whole or in part in any form by any electronic, mechanical or other means, now known or hereafter invented, including xerography, photocopying and recording, or in any information storage or retrieval system, is forbidden without the written permission of the publisher, Harlequin Enterprises Limited, 225 Duncan Mill Road, Don Mills, Ontario, Canada M3B 3K9.

All characters in this book have no existence outside the imagination of the author and have no relation whatsoever to anyone bearing the same name or names. They are not even distantly inspired by any individual known or unknown to the author, and all incidents are pure invention.

This edition published by arrangement with Harlequin Books S.A.

® and TM are trademarks of the publisher. Trademarks indicated with ® are registered in the United States Patent and Trademark Office, the Canadian Trade Marks Office and in other countries.

Printed in U.S.A.

"ARE YOU out of your mind?" Benjamin Bradley exploded, tossing the slickly produced magazine across the desk. *Texas Men* landed in the wastebasket. Bonnie Simmons Bradley bore his anger with her customary nonchalance and plucked the magazine from the leather basket. She flipped through the pages, her long, elegant fingers pausing at the section marked Texas Cowboys.

"You've made me the laughingstock of Dallas," he fumed.

"You're just angry because they called you a cowboy."

"I'm a rancher. A *rancher*," he repeated. "Four generations on the Triple Bar S, one of the oldest brands in Texas history. If anyone would understand that, I would think it would be you." Benjamin leaned forward, his gray eyes flashing. He was a handsome man, his mother thought, with strong features and a charming smile. He wasn't smiling now, though, and his dark hair needed a trim. He was a son to be proud of, virile and strong, with a temper that disappeared as quickly as it came and a sense of humor that always surprised her. He certainly didn't get that particular trait from his father.

"Blah, blah, blah," Bonnie replied, tucking a strand of silver-blond hair behind her ear. She found what she was looking for, a color photo of Benjamin as he leaned against the white fence north of the calving shed. She liked that picture. She'd taken it herself one afternoon when Benjamin thought she was merely trying to finish up a roll of film. "What difference does all that make if you're not happy?"

"I'm happy. I'm *very* happy," he insisted. "You're the one who wants me to get married, not me."

"My son, you live a boring life."

"So you put my picture in a magazine where women *shop* for men? That doesn't strike you as desperate? I can find my own women," he said, still glaring at her. "I've never had any trouble finding women."

"But not the *right* woman. I want the perfect woman for you. And don't tell me you haven't been looking, either," she added shrewdly. "You didn't have one bit of luck finding her, either. Besides, you never date anymore. You've plumb given up."

That stopped him in his tracks, Bonnie thought, hiding a smile. He didn't have a ready answer, because she, Bonnie Lynn Simmons Bradley, was absolutely correct.

He grinned suddenly and leaned back in his leather chair. "And you think the right woman, the *perfect* woman is going to write to me because she saw my picture in a magazine called *Texas Men*?"

Bonnie shrugged. It wasn't quite time to reveal the truth. "Yes, dear, I do."

His eyes narrowed. "You're calling me dear. That's a sign that you're hiding something. I thought you dragged me in here to argue about getting a new housekeeper."

"We need to replace Hattie eventually."

He shrugged. "I'm happy eating with the men in the bunkhouse."

"That won't do any longer."

"Because of this magazine crap?"

She didn't want him to know he was right. He gloated too much when he was right. "I think you should approach this 'magazine crap'—which it isn't, by the way—with an open mind, that's all."

"I don't have time for this."

"Of course you don't. I'll answer all of the letters and pick out the best ones."

"Forget it. I'm not interested in getting married. You and Dad didn't exactly set a shining example of matrimony."

"How about a little wager?" she asked softly, ignoring his protest. "Just to see what you're made of?"

Ben groaned. "Not another one of your bets. Last time it cost me one of the best brood mares I ever owned."

"How about . . . King Midas?"

"Ritter would never sell that bull."

"He might relent." Bonnie smiled, remembering the last time she'd seen her neighbor. He'd been bare-assed naked and completely satisfied.

"Let me get this straight. I go along with *this* and I get a chance to buy the bull if I *don't* find any of these magazine women acceptable?"

"I'll give you the bull myself," she said. "I'm quite sure I can find you the perfect woman. I'll expect a list of your requirements, naturally. I could probably come up with it myself, of course, but you should have some input in—"

"So all I have to do to get King Midas over here on my side of the fence is *not* marry anyone?" Ben was clearly not interested in making lists. "What's the catch?"

"No catch, dear," Bonnie said, almost purring. "Just your promise that you will entertain the women I invite out here to meet you. You will be amusing and charming and you will keep an open mind. I'll only invite the most promising candidates out to the ranch."

"You're pretty damn confident about this whole shit-for-brains plan." His eyes narrowed again. "How many?"

"Women?"

He nodded.

"Twelve?" she tried, knowing he would balk.

"One."

"Six."

"Two."

"Three," she countered, pretending chagrin.

"Three." He leaned back. "I can live with that. All I have to do is entertain three women, and then Ritter will sell King Midas?"

"Yes," Bonnie fibbed. "I'm bribing you to behave."

"I am not getting married," he repeated slowly, as if talking to a deaf person.

"We'll see," his mother said.

"All right."

He reached across the desk and shook hands with his mother.

Bonnie, satisfied with the morning's work, watched Benjamin push back the desk chair and take the magazine out of her hands. He tossed it into the wastebasket before leaving the cluttered office.

She smiled to herself. This morning's discussion had gone exactly the way she'd planned. Her son loved women, always had, though he was so damn quiet sometimes that he never quite got around to talking to them. Certainly he would fall in love with one of his houseguests. He'd managed to avoid being tied down until now, mostly because he preferred staying on the ranch to sowing wild oats in Dallas. He'd dated, of course. He wasn't exactly a monk, but none of them had been fit to be the wife of Bonnie Simmons Bradley's only child, and that's what had her worried. It was time for her very particular son to settle down. With the bride of her choosing, Bonnie thought smugly. She would drown in hell before she would let anyone less than the perfect woman marry her son.

It never crossed her mind to doubt herself. Men were simple creatures, after all. It didn't take much to please them. Hot sex, hot food and a good horse just about summed up what men wanted. She, Bonnie Simmons Bradley, could certainly come up with a woman willing to provide the first one on the list. She moved into Ben's chair and found the file marked Housekeeper. She would hire a replacement for Hattie and get the house in order for guests.

First things first.

BEN SLAPPED HIS HAT on his head and pulled the brim low. Grateful for the shade, he squinted against the hot June sun and wondered what kind of summer they were in for. He hurried toward the main barn and sanity. If his life was only half as wild and exciting as his mother thought it was, it would be pretty damn interesting. His crazy mother got some strange thoughts in that head of hers.

It was because she didn't have enough to do with herself. She'd divorced his father twenty years ago, turned the ranch over to Ben the day he turned eighteen, and moved into the city. She loved traveling, gossiping with her friends and chairing several of her favorite charitable organizations. She terrorized anyone who didn't do things her way, so Ben couldn't figure out why she was so popular.

Maybe because she was usually right. And very rich.

Ben leaned against the whitewashed fence railing and watched Jimmy's daughter break in another mare. His mother's remark about searching for the perfect woman irritated the hell out of him, and he wasn't about to go into the house until she'd driven back to Dallas.

"She gone?"

"Not yet." Ben didn't look at his top hand. Jimmy Suentes, along with most of the other ranch hands, was terrified of "the missus." According to one of the old men, Bonnie had been a holy terror since the minute she was old enough to tug on boots and head for the nearest corral.

"Think she'll be comin' out here?"

"Nope. She's got other things on her mind, like finding me a wife."

The older man chuckled and tipped his hat back. "Like spittin' in the wind, wouldn't you say?"

"Yeah." He watched for a moment, content that Lori knew what she was doing. The eighteen-year-old handled horses with a skill that everyone on the ranch respected. "She's doing a nice job. Is she still mad?"

Jimmy shrugged. "She's not buckin' the idea so much. Couple of her friends are going, too, so she's more resigned, like, than anything."

"College will be good for her."

"She couldn't go without your help. Joyce and I sure appreciate—"

"Aw, hell, Jimmy." Ben turned to his friend. "I'm happy to do it." He grinned. "I figure I'm investing in one hell of a horse trainer, if she decides to come back here and take the job after she's seen the big world."

"Darn kid thinks she's in love," Jimmy muttered.

"Again?"

"Yeah. Swears that she and the youngest Ritter boy are going to start their own business someday." They watched Lori in silence for a few minutes. The little mare pranced sideways, her nostrils flaring, but didn't protest the girl's command to trot around the ring. "I'm not real crazy about a Ritter hangin' around, but you can't tell a girl anything."

"There's too much damn matchmaking going on around here. You'd think we were 'Love Connection' or something."

"I like that show," the older man admitted. "Always makes me glad I'm a happily married man."

"You're the only one I know who is."

"Aw, you just haven't found the right woman yet, that's all. How's Bonnie gonna find you a wife?" Jimmy asked suddenly, as if he just realized what Ben had said ten minutes earlier.

Ben hesitated. Jimmy might fall off the fence laughing, but he wouldn't gossip. "She advertised. Like I was a used truck."

Jimmy's mouth gaped open, then he grinned. "How much is she askin' for ya?"

"She says if I go along and entertain a few women this summer, she'll fix it so we can get King Midas."

His friend whistled. "You have to get married to get that damn bull's sperm? You think it's worth it?"

They both knew Midas was worth just about anything. And they both knew that Ritter would rather fall in a nest of rattlers than sell his prize bull to the Triple Bar S. "I just have to be on my best behavior for a few days."

Jimmy still sounded skeptical. "You don't have to get hitched?"

"Nope. Bonnie's convinced I'll fall in love with one of 'em and want to live happily ever after."

"Could happen, I guess." He raised his voice. "Don't let her get her head down!" Lori waved and did as she was told. "Still, the apple doesn't fall far from the tree."

Ben nodded in agreement. He was his father's son, through and through. He liked horses, whiskey and women. Not necessarily in that order, of course. He could love 'em and leave 'em and not look back. He wasn't husband material, he knew that for sure.

"Where is your old man these days?"

"Vegas, I think. I haven't heard from him for a while." According to his mother, Clay Bradley had been one shit poor husband. Still Ben missed having him around the ranch. Clay knew a hell of a lot about cows and could play a mean hand of poker.

"Mebbe he'll come back for the wedding."

Ben watched the teenager hop off the mare and head toward them. "What wedding?"

"Yours." Jimmy chuckled, enjoying his own joke. "Isn't that what Miz Bradley has in mind for her only son?"

"Shut up." Ben grinned. He was safe from Bonnie's plans. There was no woman on earth who could convince him to settle down. He liked his freedom, and so far the perfect woman didn't exist who could convince him that marriage didn't mean tying a man down for life. She would have to be tall, slender, blond and blue-eyed, with legs that went up to her armpits. She'd have to know her way around a horse and she'd have to understand that the ranch came first, football second and a relationship after that. He didn't need kids and he didn't care to compromise about much of anything. He liked his coffee black, his steaks rare and his women willing.

Let his mother find a woman like that, and he might think twice.

MURIEL MADISON could have taken the summer off. After all, she was a teacher. She was supposed to have summers off, even if she'd never given herself that particular luxury. She'd tried it a couple of times but became so bored she'd gone out and gotten herself a part-time job. Something about sitting around doing nothing for ten weeks just didn't seem right.

Especially this summer. This summer was different.

Muriel allowed herself a tiny smile, then she forced her attention to the letter she'd received in this morning's mail. It was all set now. There would be no turning back once she accepted the offer. She would sublet her apartment to the neighbor's elderly mother and pack up what she needed for Rose River. A summer on a ranch sounded pretty good, especially with the salary offered. That amount of money would go a long way toward a very important winter. The house would be air-conditioned, of course, so that wouldn't be a problem. She didn't think she could work in the heat this summer. The job included cooking, nothing fancy and only for a bachelor and his infrequent guests.

And, if she found it to be too much for her, especially this summer, she would go to Christine's and make herself useful there until October 12. Magical, wonderful October 12 couldn't come soon enough. Muriel picked up the telephone and dialed the number at the bottom of the page. She was on her own now, and she was realizing that wasn't the worst thing in the world. She was going to disappear, which would make certain people very happy.

Herself included.

"Hello," she said, when a woman answered. "This is Muriel Madison. I'd like to speak to Mrs. Bradley." The arrangements were made in short order, right down to a car picking her up at the airport. Mrs. Bradley knew what she wanted and stated it clearly. By the time the phone call was finished, Muriel knew exactly what was expected of her. She turned to her empty suitcase and wondered how many clothes she should take.

It was time, she knew, to start over again. Without expecting any help from anyone, without needing anyone's help but her own. Without that silly expectation that love was forever and people kept promises.

SHE WAS THE LAST THING Ben expected. Standing on the front doorstep, her suitcases beside her, she wasn't at all what he thought he'd find. Or what his mother would have selected for him.

"Mr. Bradley?" She stuck out her right hand for him to shake, which he did. "I'm Muriel Madison." She paused, obviously waiting for him to recognize the name.

"Muriel," he said. His mother should have warned him that he was having a guest already. Tonight was the second Wednesday of the month. Poker night.

The woman frowned. He thought her eyes were brown behind the lenses of her wire-rimmed glasses. "Yes. Is Mrs. Bradley home?"

"There is no—oh, you mean my mother."

"I suppose so. Would she be the one who wrote to me?"

"Yep." Ben hesitated, warring between good sense and the vision of King Midas impregnating his heifers. "Come on in," he said, trying to sound welcoming. After all, he was a man of his word. She looked pleasant enough. Her dark curls were stuck to her forehead and, despite the pink sundress she wore, she looked hot. But she didn't complain, even picked up her own suitcases when he swung the door open wider.

"Here," he said, brushing her hands away and taking the heavy luggage. There was enough stuff in those cases to last her three weeks. He held open the door with one booted foot while she entered, then shoved the suitcases into the foyer. He liked his women tall, lean and blond. Muriel Whatever hardly reached his shoulder, and despite a heart-shaped face and delicate features, she was a little on the plump side. Still, her smile seemed nice. And the hesitant look in those maybe-brown eyes made him feel like a jerk. "I'm sorry," he said. "I guess I didn't know you were coming, uh, tonight."

"Your mother sent a car to pick me up."

"Yeah, well." He ran a hand through his dark hair. "Did she say if she was coming out here tonight?"

Muriel shook her head. "In the morning. She's supposed to give me a set of instructions and help me get started."

A set of instructions? Shit. It was worse than he thought. Ben backed up a step. God save him from overanxious females.

"Is something the matter, Mr. Bradley?"

He shook his head. Liar that he was. "Call me Ben."

"Ben." She nodded. "Call me Muriel. I think Ms. Madison is a little too formal, don't you?"

"We're pretty informal around here," he agreed. He was missing something here, all right. Maybe he should have returned Bonnie's phone calls yesterday, but he'd been busy with the new barn, and then the vet had stopped by, and one thing led to another. Damn.

"Maybe you could show me to my room." She gave him a hopeful look.

"Well, sure." Which room? Everything was pretty much a mess. A dusty, empty, comfortable mess. Where on earth was he going to put her? "How about a drink first?"

She brightened. "All right. That would be wonderful."

"Have a seat." He waved his arm toward the main room. Brown leather couches, Southwestern art and oversize coffee tables filled the living area. On one side of the room was an enormous entertainment center. Behind its doors was a thirty-one-inch television screen. The better to watch football with, of course, even though it wasn't football season. Yet.

In another corner was the wet bar. Ben strode over to it and opened doors to reveal a selection of drinks and a small sink. "You want a beer or something stronger?"

Muriel sank into one of the overstuffed leather sofas. "Something weaker, I think. Ice water?"

Well, at least she wasn't a boozer. Ben preferred a cold beer on a hot day and saved the hard stuff for after dark. He opened the small refrigerator tucked into the wall and pulled out a beer and a bottle of water for his guest.

"Thank you. I should be doing this for you," the woman said, as he handed her a glass of ice water.

That was promising. A woman who liked to wait on a man. Didn't happen much in this age, Ben figured. He sat down on the couch across from her and took a swallow of beer. He watched the woman look around the room and sigh.

"Is something wrong?" he couldn't help asking.

"No." She shook her head. "It's exactly what I expected. Your mother was very specific."

Ben took another swallow of beer. Well, she could have been more specific about his houseguest's arrival. He thought it was next weekend. He was sure he'd heard her say that. "So, ah, Muriel, are you from Texas?"

She gave him a strange look. "Yes. I grew up in Houston."

"I see. Ever been to this part of the country before?"

"Yes. I have a sister who moved to Dallas last year, so I've visited her a couple of times." She hesitated, then set the empty glass on the table. "Would you mind telling me where the bathroom is?" She smiled. "I'd like to freshen up."

"Yeah, sure." He stood, and so did she. She didn't even come to his shoulder, which made him feel awkward. He was used to tall women. He preferred a woman who could look him in the eye. Ben led her out of the living room and across the foyer, then pointed to a door on the left. "Right over there," he said.

"Thank you." She went down the hall, found the room and shut the door behind her.

Ben hurried into the living room and began a search for the portable phone. Triumphant, he lifted it from underneath a squashed corduroy pillow and quickly punched his mother's phone number. It rang twice, then launched into her answering machine message. Ben switched off the phone and tossed it into a chair. He would have to figure this out for himself.

"Mr. Bradley?" Muriel stepped into the living room.

"Ben," he said.

"Ben." She smiled again. At least she appeared good-natured. "Would you like to show me the rest of the house?"

She seemed to understand that he needed guidance, which he appreciated. "Yeah, sure." He took her across the foyer and pointed out the dining room, then took her down the west corridor. "It's just my office," he said, "and the housekeeper's room. I keep an extra guest room down here, which was originally my grandfather's room."

"Your family has lived here a long time?"

"Yep. For better or worse."

She followed him to the center of the house. "And the kitchen?"

"Here," he said. He pushed open a swinging door to reveal an enormous room at the back of the house. A pool sparkled beyond the glass windows. The kitchen had been the family's favorite gathering place when he was a child. Beyond the breakfast room was a screened porch.

Muriel looked carefully around the room. "This should do just fine," she said. "I had no idea it would be this big."

"It was the dining room before my grandmother remodeled," Ben explained. He dared a personal question. "Do you like to cook?"

She gave him a strange look. "Of course. I have a degree in home economics and a master's in education. You'll have to tell me what kind of meals you prefer."

Something was definitely wrong. Ben frowned, but Muriel didn't notice. She was too busy inspecting the stove. He watched, transfixed, as she opened the double oven doors and peered inside. She opened the refrigerator next and shook her head at its empty condition.

"I wasn't expecting—" he began, but she had already moved on to the cupboards. What in hell was she doing?

"Excuse me," he began, hoping the edge in his voice would make her stop. He didn't want a strange woman snooping around his house like this. She was supposed to make conversation, ride a horse, go out to dinner with him and be on her way. He would be polite and charming, but that was it. No one could expect anything more than that.

"Yes?" She shut the cupboard door and turned around.

"Are you hungry?"

"Not especially. Are you?"

He blinked. "You want to go out to dinner?"

Now it was her turn to blink. "Go out? Why?"

"I'm not much of a cook." This wasn't getting off to a very good start, he realized. If she was snooping through the kitchen, what would she do in the rest of the house?

"Surely you must have a freezer full of beef."

"Well, yeah, but—"

"If you'll show me, I'll figure out something for dinner." She smiled at him once again. "I might as well start right away and earn my salary."

"Salary? My mother is paying you to come here?"

Now it was Muriel's turn to look confused. "She hired me, but I assumed the owner of the house was going to be responsible for my wages. That's you, right?"

"You're the housekeeper," Ben declared, trying not to laugh. She would think he was laughing at her and not himself. Paranoid, that's what he was. Seeing his mother's conniving hand behind every person who walked through the front door.

"Yes." She looked at him as if he was insane. "Who else would I be?"

"You wouldn't believe it if I told you," Ben said, trying to control his laughter and failing. Muriel leaned against the counter and waited for him to stop. His strange behavior didn't seem to faze her in the least. When he'd caught his breath, Muriel straightened.

"I believe you already showed me the housekeeper's room," she said. "I think I'll unpack now, if you don't mind."

"I'll get your suitcases."

"Thank you. Then you can show me where the freezer is."

"I'd be right glad to, Muriel. But you don't have to worry about dinner tonight. It's poker night. The guys take turns bringing food." She looked relieved, and Ben finally noticed that she looked a little peaked. These little women didn't have much stamina. "You can take the night off."

"I think I'll rest for a few minutes," she admitted. "But I'll be glad to help with your party tonight."

He was going to get even with his mother for this. She knew he didn't need a housekeeper. She knew when he played poker. She knew he'd be home to meet the housekeeper. All of this was part of the plan to impress some strange women who read magazines advertising men. "That's not necessary, Muriel. We're real used to taking care of ourselves."

"But Mrs. Bradley said—"

He raised one hand to stop her from continuing. "Muriel, if you're going to work here, you're going to have to understand three things. One, I'm the boss. Two, you don't tell my mother anything that goes on at the ranch, and three, I don't eat peas."

"I don't have any problem with that," she said, studying him with those dark eyes. He wished she'd take her glasses off so he could see the exact color. "But tell me something." He waited for her to continue. "If you didn't know I was the new housekeeper, who did you think I was?"

He grinned at her. "Why, I figured you were my date for the weekend."

She stared at him as if she didn't believe what she'd heard. "Really?" she asked finally. "Your *date?*"

"Yep. And, according to my mother, a potential wife."

It was Muriel's turn to laugh. "You don't have to worry about that, Mr. Bradley."

"Ben," he reminded her. "And what's so funny?"

She shrugged, and he could see she was working to keep her lips from turning up into a grin. "Nothing, uh, Ben. I couldn't be farther from being wife material."

"Why not?" He couldn't imagine a woman who didn't want to get married, except his mother, who swore she'd rather be dragged from Dallas to Houston than say "I do" again.

"I'm sure you're not my type."

"And what type is that?"

She appeared to consider the question. "Well, I guess you're a little too tall, for starters. I'm already getting a neck ache just looking at you. And anyway, I would guess that you're used to dating Dallas Cowboys cheerleaders and women who used to be Miss Texas Somebody. You have that wild look about you."

He frowned. No one had ever told him he had a wild look, least of all a woman. She made him uncomfortable, and he didn't like the feeling. And he was tired of discussing his nonexistent love life with every person he conversed with. "Are you always this blunt?"

"I guess I am. But I'm a good cook, and I think that's all you should care about. Am I right?"

Ben reached for his hat, which was in the middle of the kitchen table, and put it on. "Yes, ma'am, you're one hundred percent correct. I'll get your luggage and you can settle in. I'll send Lori over and she can tell you about the house."

"Who is Lori?"

"She's the teenager who does a lot of the cleaning around here. She's earning money for college and she works by the hour. You'll have to tell her what to do, 'cause I don't care. Just as long as supper's at seven and the coffee is ready in the morning." He tried to edge toward the door. There was work to finish up before he could get ready for the game tonight, and he'd spent enough time with the hired help.

"What time do you want your coffee?"

"Set the timer on the pot for five. I get in some work before breakfast. If my eggs are ready by seven, that's good. Lunch at noon. Cold's fine. I'll even make it myself if there's stuff in the refrigerator."

"All right. I'm sure I'll have lots of questions."

"Well," he drawled, heading out of the room. "Don't ask them tonight, because I'm playing poker." Ben walked out of the room and began to whistle. He was off the hook now, free to enjoy his poker game and his freedom. Free from entertaining his mother's choice of a woman for her son.

He picked up Muriel's suitcases and carried them down the hall. He sure hoped the little woman could cook, because she certainly wasn't much to look at.

2

MURIEL AWOKE, yawned and looked around her new room. White walls, a light wood floor and a woven Navajo rug complemented the deep blue bedspread and matching curtains. The window faced the backyard and its large pool, and off to one side of the room was the door to a small private bathroom.

She didn't want to get out of the double bed. It had been such a long day. The hour-and-a-half drive to the ranch hadn't helped her stomach, either. Nerves, Muriel decided, among other things. She'd always been able to cope with life-style changes, but she was making one change after another these days.

And now she was working for a cowboy. A very handsome cowboy with a drop-dead smile and an attitude bigger than the state of Texas. She was tempted to like him, but she was tired of handsome men with nothing to offer but a mouth full of good teeth. She was tired of men, period.

Muriel looked at her watch. It was after eight, and the wide Texas sky had darkened. She would unpack her suitcases and get settled in her new home. Her new *temporary* home. This was a good place to be, she decided. She would be comfortable here. Comfortable and anonymous, with nothing to do but her job, and that seemed easy enough.

She finished unpacking quickly, then slipped on her sandals, smoothed her rumpled dress and went out into the hall. The kitchen was the first room on the right, but from the living room came the sounds of male laughter and the chink of poker chips.

"Bet 'em like you got 'em," she heard her boss holler. He sounded like he was having a good time.

"You asked for it," another man replied, then loud laughter as someone else said something Muriel was glad she couldn't hear. She ducked into the kitchen before she could be seen by the men. Somehow she didn't think a bunch of poker-playing Texans would appreciate a woman in their midst.

The scene in the kitchen didn't surprise her. Empty beer bottles, dirty glasses, uncovered cold cuts and used paper plates littered the long harvest table in the center of the room. Clearly the men had eaten already. Empty tortilla chip bags lay beside a container of salsa, and a few half-empty bottles of cola sat on the counter by the refrigerator. All in all, not too bad. The kitchen would need a good cleaning in the morning, from top to bottom. And that's what she was getting paid for.

She'd promised her sister she'd call her when she was settled, so Muriel went to the kitchen phone and dialed the familiar number. She used her calling card so the call wouldn't be billed to her employer.

"Hello?"

"Chris. It's me."

"Oh, thank goodness. I was getting worried. Are you on the ranch?"

"I'm all settled in, and it's a nice place," Muriel assured her younger sister. Chris was the one who married young and had her children early. Three babies in four years, with a husband who adored all four of them.

"You could have come here."

"Not yet. I need the money." Muriel didn't point out the obvious, that there wasn't room for one more person in that tiny house. She knew her sister would have done anything to help her.

"You could have applied for a job here in Dallas."

"Not now. I need to be on my own for a while. I'll come visit in September, and you can help me look for a place to live. Besides, who would hire me now?"

Chris sighed into the phone. "We should have been born rich."

Muriel chuckled. "Speaking of born rich, you should see this ranch. It looks like something out of a movie, and I've only seen a little bit of it."

"Is your boss nice?"

"He seems to be okay. His mother is coming out in the morning to go over the house with me. I get the feeling he's a real mama's boy. He lives alone in this ranch house, so who knows?"

"Well, you can always come here whenever you want."

"I know." Muriel turned to see Ben in the doorway. He held an empty tray in one hand and a bottle of beer in the other. "I'll call you next week," she promised, then said goodbye and hung up the phone.

"A mama's boy?" Ben repeated, setting the tray on the counter near the sink. "No one's ever called me that before."

Oops. She wasn't getting off on the right foot. Darn her big mouth. "I was just talking to my sister and letting her know I was all right."

He shook his head and dropped the beer bottle in the trash. "A mama's boy," he muttered. "You haven't met my mother yet, have you?"

"I've talked to her on the phone. She sounded as if she ran things around here."

"She'd like to," he allowed. "But she doesn't."

Muriel wasn't convinced of that particular fact, but she knew when to keep her mouth shut. "Okay."

"I make all the decisions around here," he insisted. "Ask anyone."

"I believe you." She opened the cupboard and found the jar of peanut butter she'd seen earlier. "You don't mind if I make myself a sandwich, do you?"

He frowned. "Of course not. This is your kitchen."

"I'll make a grocery list tomorrow, and you can point me toward the nearest supermarket."

"You have your choice of cars," he said. "The station wagon or the truck."

"Where do you keep the bread?"

He reached for a deep drawer and slid it open. "In here, last I looked."

"Thanks." She found the silverware drawer and made herself a sandwich while Ben watched. "Don't let me keep you from your game."

"I'm sitting this one out. Trying to change my luck."

"Oh." He was starting to make her nervous.

"You don't look much like a housekeeper. You're too young."

"I'm almost thirty."

His eyebrows rose. "You look younger."

"It's because I'm short." She took a bite of the sandwich, then opened the refrigerator and retrieved a carton of milk. She hoped it was fresh.

"Can you make chicken-fried steak?"

"I can, but it's not good for you." Muriel located the cupboard with the glasses inside, then poured herself a glass of milk.

"What in hell does that have to do with anything?"

"You're not getting any younger. You should start watching your cholesterol." She hadn't realized how hungry she was, or how hard it was to talk with peanut butter stuck to the roof of her mouth.

"What are you, a nurse?"

"Home economics teacher, with a specialty in nutrition."

"Oh, Lord." He rolled his eyes heavenward. "I want eggs and bacon in the morning, with biscuits and butter and maybe some homemade jam."

"You're the boss," she said, finishing the glass of milk. "You can die young if you want to."

"Thanks." He started to back out of the kitchen. "I appreciate your cooperation. Now I'm going back to my game."

A shorter man poked his head into the kitchen. "Ben! You in this hand?" His dark eyes widened when he saw Muriel, and he nodded. "Ma'am," was his tentative greeting. He looked as if he wished he had a hat to tip. He looked as if Ben had a woman and hadn't told anyone.

"Hello," Muriel tried, hoping to erase the shocked look on his face.

Ben hid a smile and hurried to explain. "Meet the new cook and housekeeper, Jimmy. Muriel here is going to watch my cholesterol for me."

"Pleased," the man said, still wearing a surprised expression. "Lori—that's my daughter—will be real happy to make your acquaintance."

"She will?"

"Yes, ma'am. She's been doin' some of the cleanin' around here, and I can't say as it puts her in a good mood."

"I'll be glad to meet her, too."

"Jimmy runs things around here for me," Ben explained. "We've been together on this ranch a long time. He lives in one of the houses out back."

The older man attempted to back out of the room, and Ben let him.

"Good luck," Muriel called as Ben started to follow his friend. "I hope you win."

He winked at her. "Yes, ma'am, I'll do my best."

With that he was gone, and Muriel breathed a sigh of relief. Ben Bradley was tall, dark and handsome. He was a flirt, too. He was exactly the kind of man she should avoid. His mother said he was pretty much a recluse, but that was going to change. Muriel hadn't asked what she'd meant by that statement. It wasn't her business. But Mrs. Bradley had continued, and said that her son would be entertaining on weekends, that the house should be clean and the food good. Muriel had assured her that wasn't a problem.

She finished her sandwich, wiped her hands on a paper napkin and put her glass in the dishwasher. She eyed the mess on the table, then gathered the cold cuts and wrapped them in plastic before putting them in the refrigerator. Surely the men would know where to look if they wanted more to eat. She dumped the trash into the garbage can, wiped crumbs off the counter and put the rolls into their bag to stay fresh. She put the dirty dishes in the dishwasher and fixed the coffeepot before she left the kitchen.

In the morning she would find the teenager who did the heavy work, meet Mrs. Bradley and plan her meals. This job was going to be a piece of cake.

"WELL, HOT DAMN, Ben! I think that pot's mine." Jimmy swept the chips across the table and piled them up in front of him. "Must be my lucky night."

"It sure ain't mine," a skinny cowboy muttered.

"Mine, either." Ben shook his head. "Don't know what's wrong with me tonight. I can't even deal *myself* a good hand."

"I think you're doin' all right. You could've warned me about the woman, though," Jimmy grumbled. "Never thought I'd be walkin' into one in the kitchen. Thought you had somethin' goin' on you wasn't telling me about."

"As if I could get away with anything around here." He cut the cards for the ranch hand on his left. The other men stayed quiet. Ben was sure they were wondering where this conversation was going. Whatever happened would make real good gossip in the morning. Cowboys sure liked to gossip.

"She's a sweet-looking little thing," Jimmy added.

The men's gazes turned to Ben, who ignored them and waited for the cards to be dealt. He didn't want to discuss the woman. It didn't seem right. He looked around the table at the expectant faces and had to relent. "She's the new housekeeper," he announced. "Name's Muriel. You can call her Miss Madison. I don't think she's married. And I don't want her hassled by a bunch of horny old cowhands."

"We ain't old," one retorted, and the others laughed and picked up their cards.

Ben grimaced. It looked like it was going to be a long summer.

MURIEL HATED MORNINGS. She wondered how she could live through another one. She wondered when the sickness would ever stop. She'd stopped wondering if there was anything she could do to stop the queasy feeling that too often erupted into losing her breakfast.

She felt sorry for herself in the mornings, and that was just as pathetic as hanging her head over the toilet bowl, Muriel decided. She reached for a washcloth, wiped her face and then, when her knees stopped trembling, stood at the sink and brushed her teeth. Dark eyes and pale skin looked back at her. Muriel made a face and took a deep breath. At least she'd managed to shower and dress before the nausea hit, and this had to stop eventually. Everyone said it should, but it wasn't stopping soon enough to fry eggs and bacon for her boss's breakfast.

She gulped and tried to breathe through her mouth and think about something else. Like Christmas. Christmas was at least six months away, but it was certainly something to look forward to this year. She and Christine had it all planned.

Muriel straightened, washed her hands and headed to the kitchen. If she wanted to keep this job she was going to have to fry eggs. And she was going to have to do it without throwing up.

Her boss was in the kitchen when she returned. He had his head bent over the newspaper, and he didn't look up when she entered the room. He'd poured his own coffee, thank goodness, and judging from the marks of perspiration on the back of his shirt, he looked as if he'd been outside already and done half a day's work.

"Good morning," she said, trying to sound perky.

"Mornin'." He looked toward her for a second, then went back to his paper.

"What do you want for breakfast?" She dreaded the answer and she started hunting for the frying pan before he gave it.

"Four eggs, over easy. Five strips of bacon and three pieces of toast if you don't have biscuits."

"No biscuits right now," she said. "But I can make some."

"Don't bother. Toast is fine."

Toast was about all she could look at. Muriel found eggs and bacon in the refrigerator, then prayed for the willpower to cook them. Maybe if she didn't watch too closely and did that mouth-breathing technique she would be all right. No one was going to want a cook who couldn't cook.

She peeled off the strips of bacon and set them in the cast-iron skillet, then put the skillet on the front burner and turned it on. She flipped the switch on the exhaust fan above the stove and prayed it would take out most of the smell before her stomach objected.

"Looks like another hot day," Ben said.

Muriel obediently turned and looked out the window at the blue sky. "Yes, it does."

"You look like you could use some sun."

"I'm, uh, naturally pale," she said, turning to poke the bacon with the spatula. It crackled and spit, so she turned the heat down a little.

"In fact, you look like a damn—darn ghost. Sure you're not sick?"

"I've been a little under the weather lately," she admitted, hoping to sound casual. "But I'm feeling fine now."

"Burn the bacon."

"What?"

"Burn the bacon," he repeated. "I like it black and crunchy."

"Oh. Sure." She turned the heat back up and fussed with the frying bacon until it looked charred. Then she found a plate to put it on, dabbed it with paper towels, then drained most of the grease into a bowl. She held her breath, cracked four eggs into the skillet and closed her eyes as they spread and sizzled in the pan. She moved away from the stove and put bread in the toaster.

"Dump some salsa over those eggs, all right?" He went back to his paper.

Muriel turned and picked up the spatula again. She flipped the eggs, counted to ten, then flipped them onto the plate. There was half a jar of salsa in the refrigerator, and she dumped most of it on top of the eggs. The toast popped up, and she piled that on the plate and brought the food to her boss. It took her a moment to get the silverware together, and by the time she brought him a knife and fork, Ben had folded his paper and was eyeing his breakfast with appreciation.

"Thank you, Muriel."

"You're welcome." She swallowed hard as he speared the egg with his fork and the yolk ran yellow against the other eggs and mixed with the green chili salsa.

"You must have a cast-iron stomach."

"Yep."

"Anything else?"

"More coffee?"

"Sure." She refilled his coffee cup without looking at his plate.

"You're not eating?"

"No."

He looked surprised. He probably figured she was on a diet. "What happened to your last cook?"

He gestured toward the empty chair across from him. "Sit down." Muriel did, then he answered her question. "She retired. Hattie was about ninety years old, I think. She broke her hip and decided to go live with her daughter in Dallas a few months ago."

"Who's been doing the cooking?"

"No one. I've been eating with the men. Jimmy's wife runs a pretty good chow hall."

The next question was an obvious one. "Then why did you hire me?"

"My mother did." Ben paused to spear another piece of egg. "Seems that I'm entertaining this summer. That's where you come in."

"Mrs. Bradley said that you were going to have a lot of company."

He winced. "Mrs. Bradley has some pretty damn strange ideas. And I'm sure she'll be here soon to explain them to you. Just nod, pretend you're going along with everything she says, then ignore it."

"Ignore it?"

"Yep." He looked up at her and winked. "That's the best way to handle my mother, trust me. Pretend to go along. It'll save you a lot of trouble."

"Okay."

Interesting advice. Muriel eyed the handsome rancher and wondered why he wasn't married already. Maybe his mother scared off any women that got too close to her son.

"I WANT HIM MARRIED," the blond woman declared. "That's where you come in."

Muriel sat down. She'd been summoned from the kitchen by Ben's mother, led to the office and shown a seat in front of a wide mahogany desk. "You want *who* married, Mrs. Bradley?"

"My son. He could have continued to eat at the bunkhouse, of course. He could continue to act like a hermit, too." She sighed, then turned a blue-eyed gaze toward Muriel. "This summer is going to change things."

Obviously the mother and son shared a certain bluntness. Muriel waited for the woman to explain. "Which is why you hired me?"

"Yes. You're going to see that the house is kept in order, that the meals are edible, that things run smoothly when our guests are here. I want them to understand that the ranch is a home, after all. I want us to look our best."

Muriel had no idea what the woman was talking about, but she nodded as if she understood. *Pretend to go along.* That had been Ben's advice. "When is he getting married?"

"I'm not sure. He'll fall in love with one of them, I'm sure. I know exactly what kind of woman he likes. I've been...careful." She tapped a glossy magazine with her fingernail. "There've been so many from which to choose. If the first set doesn't work, I'll keep trying."

Insanity could run in the family, Muriel thought. All those generations working in the hot Texas sun could have whithered the gene pool down to this.

"You're awfully young," Bonnie Bradley muttered. "I was hoping you'd be more maternal looking. Your qualifications were those of someone older."

"Mrs. Bradley, I am definitely maternal. And older than I look."

"You're not his type anyway." She tapped the magazine again. "The first one arrives next Friday. Make sure the upstairs guest room is ready for her. Put her in the room next to Ben. Make it easy for him." She smiled. "Are we clear?"

"Perfectly." It was clear that the people on this ranch were nuts.

"Good."

Muriel rose, anxious to get back to the kitchen. She'd been in the middle of cataloging supplies when Mrs. Bradley found her.

"Lori Suentes will continue doing the heavy work. She's yours twelve hours a week until she leaves for college."

"You are aware that I'm taking this job for only four months?"

"Yes. Which works out fine. The next Mrs. Bradley will want to choose her own staff, I'm sure." Mrs. Bradley consulted her notes and continued. "You'll have Sundays off, of course, unless there's company, in which case you'll have Monday as your day off instead. And Thursday afternoons. You might combine that with a trip to town, so that mornings are spent buying supplies. We have accounts at several stores. I'll give you a list."

"That sounds fine."

"Good. One more thing, Miss Madison." Muriel waited. "Cowboys are real flirts. Don't sleep with any of them, and if you decide to marry one of them, know what you're getting into before you make a big mistake."

"I have no intention of getting married, Mrs. Bradley." Truer words were never spoken.

Bonnie Bradley raised her beautiful eyebrows. "Then you're a very smart woman." She rose. "Now I'll show you the rest of the house."

Muriel kept a straight face. "Thank you." If only Mrs. Bradley knew how safe the cowboys were. She was no femme fatale at her best, and now—well, she was definitely any man's worst nightmare.

MURIEL RETURNED to the kitchen as soon as the tour of the house was finished. It was a simple home, with the second story holding bedrooms and bathrooms. Determined to shop for groceries, she'd returned to continue with her list of food. Lori Suentes and her mother, a kind-looking woman with a pleasant expression, came over to the house first. They knocked on the side door and came down the hall to introduce themselves.

"Welcome, Muriel," Joyce Suentes said in a soft voice. "I hope you'll be happy working here."

"Thank you. It's nice to meet you," Muriel said, not quite certain what was expected. "Can I get you some coffee or iced tea?"

Joyce shook her head. "We just came over to say hello."

Muriel turned to the young girl. Lori was a wiry teenager, with long dark hair and gray eyes. "And I understand you're my helper around here."

"Ben said you'll still need me here in the house," the girl said. She didn't sound particularly enthused about it.

"Yes," Muriel said, accustomed to moody teenage girls. "Do you like to work in the morning or afternoon?"

"I have a choice?" Muriel nodded. The girl look relieved. "I'm with the horses in the afternoon, and I have a job waitressing at night."

"Mornings, then. How about coming over around nine and we'll work out a schedule?"

Lori smiled, and Muriel realized how attractive the girl was. "Okay."

"You'll have to fill me in on how everything works around here."

"That's easy," the girl said. "Ben doesn't really care as long as there's food on the table when he wants to eat."

"I got that impression."

Joyce chuckled. "You know how men are."

Muriel didn't. She thought she had, but she'd been wrong. "Does your husband work here?"

"Yes. We live north of the big barns, in the small white house with the blue door. My Jimmy's parents worked here, too. We've been here for as long as I can remember. Let me know if there's anything I can do to help you," the woman offered, ushering her daughter out of the kitchen.

"Thanks." Muriel went back to her list. At least she was getting organized. She'd take a car and head to town soon. She'd feel better when she knew she had everything she needed to do her job. Judging from the mess in the sink, Ben had found last night's cold cuts and made himself a sandwich while Muriel had been with his mother.

Muriel finished her list and fixed herself a sandwich, too. Mrs. Bradley was nowhere to be seen. She'd headed toward the barn after showing Muriel the house. It was none of her business if the woman was a little eccentric. Muriel was content to entertain Princess Diana or Phyllis Diller, as long as one of the crazy Bradleys paid her salary every month.

"ALREADY?" Ben roared. "You fixed it up already?"

"Of course," a woman drawled. "Why not?"

Muriel stepped outside into the hot Texas wind. She carried her purse and her list and had hoped to find keys in the station wagon. Actually, she'd hoped to find someone to ask about taking the car to town. She hadn't expected Ben and his mother to be standing toe-to-toe in the driveway.

"Excuse me?" she tried, but neither paid the least bit of attention to her.

"Well, you didn't waste any time," he said, putting his hands on his jeaned hips.

"Of course not." Bonnie tossed her purse into the powder-blue convertible and opened the car door. Her son blocked her way.

"I'll take the bet back."

"You can't. You already agreed." She stepped around him, slid behind the steering wheel and shut her car door with a satisfied click. "She arrives tomorrow. You can send her home on Sunday." She winked at him. "That is, if you want to."

"I'll want to," he growled, stepping back from the car as if he was afraid she would mow him down.

Bonnie slipped on a pair of overlarge sunglasses, then drove around the circular driveway until she reached the long road that would take her to the highway. Dust swirled behind the car, and the engine roared.

Ben turned and saw Muriel standing in the driveway. He tipped back his head, but he didn't smile. "You need something?"

"A car. I'm going to town to buy food."

He pointed toward a shiny black pickup. "Get in. I'm heading there myself."

"You really don't have to—"

"I'm going," he said. "Get in. No sense taking two cars to the same place."

"You're the boss," she said, following him to the truck.

"Yeah." He pulled the brim of his hat lower and went around to the driver's side of the truck. "That's what I think, too."

He turned on the engine, flipped the air-conditioning to high. Then he backed the truck out of the driveway and headed down the dusty road. But when they reached the main road, he turned left instead of right. The land was flat and golden brown, with nothing to see but distant oil wells. They drove in silence for long minutes while Muriel looked out the window and pretended to be interested in the scenery. What there was of it.

"This is all Triple Bar S land," Ben said finally.

"Must be a big ranch."

"One of the biggest. Uncle Jack found oil back in the thirties, so we haven't had to worry much about making a profit on cows."

"Oh."

"But I like cows."

She assumed he liked cows or he wouldn't have a cattle ranch, but she didn't point that out. She wondered how fast they were going. Her stomach rolled, and she swallowed hard. "I'm not in a big hurry to get to the store," she said, hoping he would take the hint.

He didn't. His booted foot didn't ease up on the gas pedal. "Do you know much about women?"

She stared at him, but he kept his gaze on the empty road ahead of them. "I think so," she replied, wondering if she could laugh and still keep her job.

"What do women want in a man?"

"I'm not sure what you mean."

He shot her a disgusted look. "What do women want, when they meet a man for the first time? Like on a first date?"

"Well, you hope he's clean." It was a feeble joke, but Ben didn't smile.

"Yeah?"

"Sure. And you want someone with good manners. Someone who can talk intelligently."

Ben nodded. "That's what I thought. Talking has never worked real well for me. Anything else?"

Muriel gripped the dashboard. "You hope he's a good driver and doesn't go so fast that you end up upside-down in a Texas ditch."

He glanced toward her and nodded. He lifted his foot from the gas pedal and slowed down to seventy-five. "Yes, ma'am. Anything else?"

Loyalty. Fidelity. Honesty. Commitment. "Not that I can think of. Not for the first date, anyway."

"If you think of anything, let me know. I've got a woman coming tomorrow."

"Congratulations. Someone special?"

He frowned. "I sure hope not."

"Surely you've been out on dates before." He looked like a man who knew his way around women. He just had that look.

"I sure as hell don't invite women to my home," he grumbled. "And I don't date women someone else picked out for me, either."

Muriel eased her death grip on the dashboard. "How far away is the nearest town?"

"About twenty miles."

They'd probably flown over fifteen of them already, she decided. "Is there anything special you want for the weekend, like a romantic dinner for two?"

"Hell, no."

"I thought you wanted to impress her."

Ben thought about that for a long moment. "Okay, Muriel. Go ahead. Make a romantic dinner for tomorrow night. Give it your best shot, just don't cook anything—"

"Green," she finished for him.

"Yeah." He smiled at her. "You catch on pretty quick."

He didn't know the half of it. Vegetables she could handle. Men she couldn't.

3

"HOW ABOUT A BEER?" Ben helped Muriel fill the back of the truck with brown bags of groceries. He decided he could use a cold one after his meeting with the local cattlemen's association. A longer-winded group of men didn't exist anywhere in Texas.

He'd worked up quite a thirst, and he noticed that Muriel's dark curls were plastered to her forehead and her cheeks were pink. The extra color looked good on her. He wondered what she looked like without her glasses. She had a cute nose, and when she smiled her face lit up.

"Well—"

"You don't have to drink beer," he said. "You can have a Coke."

"Okay." She looked resigned, but Ben figured she'd perk up after she had something to drink. Sloppy Joe's was dark and quiet on a Thursday afternoon, which was fine with Ben. He'd had enough noise for one day. He opted for a table instead of a stool at the bar and tilted his hat off his forehead as the waitress approached.

"What can I get you folks?"

"A Coke, please," Muriel said. "With lots of ice, if you have it."

"And a beer. Lone Star's fine."

The waitress brought their drinks and left them alone. Ben was content to sit in the dim lounge and nurse his beer. He didn't think his new housekeeper could complain about spending her first afternoon on the job relaxing at Sloppy Joe's.

"I have frozen food in the truck," Muriel said. "I really should get back."

"All right," he agreed, but didn't move.

"I planned all the meals for the next week," she said. She reached into her purse and pulled out a piece of paper. "Do you want to go over the menu?"

"Now, why would I want to do that?"

"In case there is something you don't—"

"Forget it. Run the house any way you want. I thought we settled that."

She looked disappointed, as if she'd hoped for some kind of talk about recipes, but she tucked the paper into her purse. "Who is your guest this weekend?"

"I don't know. Bonnie invited her."

Muriel tried to hide her look of surprise.

"Yeah, I know," Ben said. "It sounds pretty damn dumb, doesn't it?"

"I guess your mother can invite anyone she wants to the ranch."

"Ever heard of a magazine called *Texas Men*?"

Muriel shook her head.

"It's a magazine with men in it. You can write to them. It's a matchmaking service." Muriel waited for him to continue. "My mother put me in it," he said, trying to keep the frustration out of his voice.

Her eyes widened. "You're kidding."

"Nope. Bonnie wants me to get married, and she figures she's going to help the process along."

"Do you want to get married?"

"No way in hell, lady. I'm not the marrying kind. Never will be."

She looked as if she believed him. "So why are you going along with this?"

He decided against telling anyone but Jimmy about King Midas. "To make my mother happy. If she gets this out of her system then she'll leave me alone."

"There's nothing wrong with getting married. And there's nothing wrong with meeting new people. Surely your mother wouldn't subject you to women you had nothing in common with."

"God only knows what she would do."

Muriel smiled. "I think it sounds interesting."

"I hope you still think so after you're through cooking for them."

"It's romantic, too."

"Romantic?" He winced. "Only a woman would think that."

"Obviously not, or there wouldn't be magazines full of men looking for love."

He thought about that for a second, then drained his glass. "Maybe, Muriel, but I'm not one of them." He tossed a ten on the table, then got up and pushed his chair back. "Guess we'd better get you and your frozen food to the ranch." He touched her back and guided her toward the door.

"Lori and I have a lot to do to get ready for tomorrow. What time do you think this woman will arrive?"

Ben opened the door and followed Muriel into the dusty parking lot. "I don't know. Bonnie isn't wasting any time, so our guest could be here first thing in the morning."

"Maybe you'll like her."

He shrugged. "Maybe I will. Doesn't matter if I do or I don't." He climbed inside the truck and waited for Muriel to haul herself onto the front seat and shut the door.

He was stuck with this plan, and he couldn't do anything but go along with it.

He swung the truck onto the road. "You ever been married, Muriel?"

"No."

"Ever wanted to be?"

She seemed to hesitate. "Yes. But it didn't work out. What about you?"

"Never wanted to be," he admitted. "My folks fought from sunup to sundown without taking a breath. I figured that was a good thing to stay away from, myself."

"Are they divorced?"

"Yep. For a long time now."

"Does he work on the ranch?"

"No." Ben chuckled. "The ranch belonged to my mother's family. My dad was a cowboy who married the boss's daughter. It was a match made in hell."

"Where is he now?"

"Vegas, last I heard. He'll be coming up for Labor Day weekend, for the barbecue. You'll get to meet him then." Ben stepped on the gas and urged the truck toward home. He could still get in a few hours of work before sundown, if he was lucky. Muriel could grip the dashboard and turn pale if she wanted to, but she was going to have to get used to Texas speed. He glanced at her. She was a cute little thing, despite the glasses that made her look more like a college professor than a cook. She wore no jewelry, and her nails were short.

Too bad she wasn't blond. He liked to look at blondes.

"Hi," THE YOUNG WOMAN SAID. A limousine driver piled her luggage behind her, then hurried to his car. "I'm Tessie Mae Gibbons. I believe I'm expected?"

"Of course. Come on in." The houseguest had arrived. Tessie Mae looked like a man's dream come true, Muriel decided, as she ushered the young beauty through the front door of the house. Wearing a formfitting white dress that stopped just above her knees, the woman had a body that would rival any *Playboy* model. The buttons on her bodice were unbuttoned enough to show off a deep cleavage. A tiny diamond heart-shaped necklace nestled against her collarbone.

"Thank you," Tessie Mae purred. Platinum hair lay in shiny waves past her shoulders, her big eyes were the color of blueberries, and her skin was peaches-and-cream perfection. Muriel figured Ben would faint dead away with pleasure. Any man would.

"Have a seat," Muriel said, wiping her hands on her apron. She'd found a pile of thick cotton aprons in the linen closet and was pleased to wear one over her baggy jeans. She'd have to buy new clothes soon. "I'll tell Ben that you've arrived."

"Why, thank you. And you are?" She sat on the couch and crossed her legs. Her white high heels showed off perfect legs. And Tessie Mae knew it, too.

"Miss Madison. The housekeeper. Can I get you something to drink?"

Tessie Mae's full pink lips turned up in a smile. "Why, I'd like that *so* much. Thank you."

Muriel waited, but Tessie didn't elaborate on what she'd like so much. "Tea, coffee, soda pop? Something stronger?"

"Do you have any lemonade? With lots of ice and just a *twist* of mint?" She smiled, a gracious princess asking a favor. "I would dearly *love* some, if you have it. But don't go to any trouble on my account."

"I'll see what I can do," Muriel said, wondering where she was going to find fresh mint leaves. "Make yourself comfortable."

"But what about my luggage? Can someone bring it in?"

"I'll see that it's taken care of."

The blue eyes darkened. "I don't want my cosmetics to melt out there in the hot sun."

"I'll take care of it," Muriel repeated. This one was used to having her own way. Muriel left the living room, went to the front door and tugged the heavy tapestry cases inside the foyer. There. The princess's makeup wouldn't melt now.

"What the hell are you doing?" Ben appeared behind her and took the cases out of her hand. "You're going to hurt yourself."

"Maybe I'm stronger than I look."

"I doubt it." He lifted the cases easily and set them against the wall. "I take it our houseguest has arrived."

"She's in the living room. Waiting for her lemonade."

"Well?" Ben lowered his voice. "What am I in for?"

"Every man's dream," Muriel whispered, and watched his face light up.

"Really?"

"Really. You'll be in love within five minutes. Maybe less."

"You teasing me, Muriel?"

"No." Muriel tried not to laugh out loud. He was the easiest-tempered man she'd ever met. She hoped Tessie Mae would be gentle with him. "Your mother may have done you a favor."

"That'll be the day," he grumbled, but he didn't waste any time heading around the corner to the living room.

It took a few minutes to whip up some lemonade from a can of frozen concentrate. She dumped a lot of ice in a tall glass, ignored the request for mint leaves and hurried to the living room to watch the show. Despite his complaining, Ben surely wouldn't mind entertaining the lovely Tessie for the weekend.

"I'll saddle up Angel and we'll go for a ride," Ben was saying.

Tessie pursed her pretty lips. "I don't know. I'm a little afraid of animals that big." She held out her hand for the lemonade glass, and Muriel handed it to her. Tessie never took her eyes from Ben's face.

"Angel's very safe," he assured her. "Every kid on the ranch has learned to ride on her." He looked every inch the Texas cowboy, with his dusty boots, worn jeans and lightweight denim shirt. He was as handsome as a cowboy could be, too, Muriel noted. And Tessie Mae was soaking it all in. Who could blame her? Some women found all that Western testosterone irresistible.

"Could we go *very* slow?"

Ben smiled, his eyes dropping briefly to Tessie's long legs. "Why, that's exactly the way I like to do everything."

Muriel cleared her throat, and Ben looked up. "Can I get you a drink?"

He nodded toward a glass of water. "Got it, thanks. Is Tessie's room ready?"

"Yes."

"I'll take her bags up there, then." He stood and gave his hand to Tessie as if she wasn't capable of standing by herself. Tessie blushed becomingly. "You can change into riding clothes," he said, "and I'll give you a tour of the ranch."

Tessie left her empty glass on the coffee table and swept out of the room like a queen. Muriel watched as Ben hurried after her. Men were strange creatures. She was glad she was through with them.

"YOU'VE GOT TO HELP ME," Ben whispered. Muriel shut the oven door and turned around to see a desperate expression on her boss's face.

"What's the matter?"

"I can't take a weekend of this."

"Of what? Miss Gorgeous not falling for your charm?"

He looked chagrined. "I spent all afternoon with her. Which is enough for a lifetime, by the way."

"She seems nice." *If you like the type.*

"I don't care how nice she is. She's afraid of horses. She's afraid of dogs. She's probably afraid of barns, too, I don't know. I do know she's driving me crazy."

"She's stunning."

"Yeah. She was Miss Texas three years ago. Not bad."

"Not bad? That's all you can say?"

"Contrary to what you believe, I do not sleep with every woman that bats her eyelashes at me." He stopped, as if thinking. "At least, not until now. I get the feeling that the minute I get her clothes off, she's going to slap a marriage certificate on the pillow."

Muriel picked up a spoon and stirred her gravy. "Poor man. You have a beautiful ex-Miss Texas at your house for the weekend. Life is tough."

"I don't want to take any chances," he muttered. "One wrong step and I'd be walking down the aisle."

"So what do you expect me to do about it?"

"Poison her?"

Muriel gave him a withering look. "I've only worked for you for two days and you're asking me to commit murder?" She started to chuckle. He was an outrageous man, but he made her laugh.

"We're in this together," he reminded her. "Your job is to protect me."

"Not from what your mother says."

"You're supposed to protect me from her, too." He leaned against the counter. "What are we having for dinner?"

"Something romantic. In the dining room." She looked at his dusty jeans. "You'd better change."

He shook his head. "No way. She wanted to meet a cowboy, she's going to eat with one."

"You smell like a horse."

"That's fine. I'm supposed to."

"Well, stand back from me a little bit. I don't want dust in my gravy."

"Smells good."

"Better than you."

"You know, Muriel, you're going to make a damn good cook around here."

"Thanks." If he only knew cooking his eggs made her sick to her stomach each morning. "I like to cook."

"One thing."

"What?"

"Your name. Muriel. That's a mouthful."

"That's my name."

"You need a nickname."

"I need you out of my kitchen," she said, nudging him away from a drawer. She opened it and pulled out a whisk.

"Mel," he stated. "How about that?"

"I really don't care," Muriel said, but she looked over at him to see if he was teasing her. "Do you really think I need a nickname?"

"Everyone has one."

"What do they call you, then?"

"Boss." He winked at her. "What else?"

"I'm not sure I want to be called Mel. It sounds like a man's name."

"No, it doesn't. I don't want to have to say Mew-ree-ell all the time when Mel is faster."

Muriel thought it over. Actually, having a cowboy nickname was appealing. A new name for a new life. "Okay. Mel it is."

"Okay, Mel. How do I get my houseguest to leave?"

"You don't. How long is she staying?"

"Till Sunday. Her flight back to Galveston is at three."

"I'm having a hard time feeling sorry for you."

"You haven't been around Tessie Mae for the past three hours. This isn't going to work out, believe me. I could have an emergency. During dinner you could come in and say that I had to go to the hospital."

Muriel ignored him and peeked in the oven. The roast was browning nicely. "Your mother called."

"Shit."

"She said to tell you she hoped you would have a wonderful weekend and she'll be out on Sunday morning to meet your guest. She suggested I serve brunch at eleven."

"Ben?" a sweet voice called. Tessie peeked into the kitchen. "I'm so sorry to bother you," she said, her little voice husky. "I've been waiting for you in the living room. Did you forget about me?"

"No, darlin'," Ben said. He smiled a completely charming smile and let his gaze sweep her from head to toe. "You look like the yellow rose of Texas."

"Thank you." She pirouetted, showing off the pale yellow dress that clung to her curves. "I'm glad y'all like it."

"Oh, I do," he assured her. "Let me fix you a drink."

"Well…" She pretended to hesitate. "Maybe just a *tiny* one."

"How about a little whiskey and soda to whet your appetite?"

"I would *love* it."

He swept her out of the kitchen without a backward look at Muriel. She watched him go, amazed that he could flirt like that one minute when before Tessie walked in he'd been trying to figure out how to get the woman out of his house. No wonder women got in trouble. Men lied. Men lied *easily*.

Muriel patted the slight bulge underneath her apron. Boy or girl, she would raise this child to be honest.

TESSIE CAUSED a small commotion Saturday morning when she strolled to the main corral for her riding lesson. She wore skintight white jeans with a pink tank top stretched over her ample chest. She had every hand within sight sauntering over to the corral for a closer look.

Lori passed her on her way to the house. "You have to see this, Miss Mel," the girl said. "That woman is making the men crazy."

"I can imagine." Muriel chuckled and finished wiping the kitchen counter. She'd served a light breakfast in the dining room and watched Ben try to drink his coffee and answer questions about horses at the same time. "Ben is going to teach her how to ride."

"This I've got to see," Lori said. "Come on. Let's watch."

Muriel was tempted. A quick peek out the window showed a crowd gathering. "I think Tessie Mae is afraid of horses."

"She's not afraid of men," the teenager pointed out. "She's showing off everything she's got, and I think what she's got isn't what she started out with."

"Implants?"

"Sure. They sure stick out straight, don't they?"

Muriel considered the question. "I guess so, but I don't think it matters to the men here on the ranch."

"Of course not, but I'd like to see those white jeans hit the dust."

"You have a wicked streak, young lady."

Lori grinned. "I'm only saying what we're both thinking." She edged closer to the window. They saw the ranch hands crowding against the railing of the fence. "Come on. Let's watch the show."

Muriel untied her apron and tossed it over the back of a chair. "Just for a few minutes," she cautioned. She still had supper to plan for the evening, and Tessie Mae had whispered that she hoped supper would have less fat and more vegetables because, unlike some people, *she* had to watch her figure. A pointed look at Muriel had followed, leaving Muriel briefly reconsidering the issue of poison.

Lori was already out the door, so Muriel had to hurry to keep up. They followed the path from the side of the house, past the bushes that lined the pool area, and through the maze of corrals and barns that comprised the main part of the home place, as Ben referred to it.

A weathered older man, his skin dark from the sun, tilted his hat back and smiled as Lori approached. "Come to see the show?"

"Wouldn't miss it." Lori gestured for Muriel to come closer. "Miss Mel, you haven't met my daddy yet, have you?"

"As a matter of fact, I have. At the poker game." Muriel shook the man's hand.

"Pleased to see you're finding your way around the ranch," he said, smiling.

"I'm trying," Muriel said. "I'm really glad to have Lori working with me. Your daughter is going to be a big help to me this summer."

"She's a worker, no doubt about that," he agreed. A shout came up from some of the men by the barn, so Jimmy turned to look. "Guess Miss Texas is about to ride a horse," he drawled, making room at the fence for Lori and Muriel. "This oughter be pretty damn interestin'."

"Why is everyone watching this?"

"Well, Miz Mel, it's not often that we have Miss Texas out here at the ranch. Ben doesn't entertain much." He grinned as Ben, leading a palomino mare, entered the corral. Tessie Mae simpered at his side. White boots sparkled with rhinestones as she walked into the middle of the corral and waved to the boys on the fence.

"Hi, there!" she called. Her makeup was perfect, her lipstick a shade darker than her top.

No one answered. Muriel figured the sight of that tank top had paralyzed their vocal cords. Ben said something to her, and she turned and put one sparkling booted foot in the stirrup. Ben helped her lift her tightly covered rump into the saddle while a couple of recovered cowhands shouted, "Go get 'er, boss!"

The mare stepped sideways, and Tessie Mae let out a little yelp. Ben looked disgusted, but he showed his guest how to hold the reins, then proceeded to lead her around the corral so she would grow accustomed to the feel of the horse. When he headed toward Muriel, he raised his eyebrows.

"What are you ladies doing here?" he asked.

"Watching a riding lesson," Lori replied, not bothering to hide her grin. "We wouldn't have missed this for anything."

Tessie frowned. "Ben? Are you stopping so soon?"

Ben handed the reins to Lori. "Here, honey. You take over for a few minutes while I get my horse saddled up."

Lori gave him a dirty look, but she hopped off the fence and did as she was told. She led a frowning Tessie Mae away from Ben and past a lineup of appreciative cowboys.

"Mel," Ben said, tipping his hat. "Mighty fine breakfast this morning."

"Thanks. Glad you enjoyed it."

"I'm real surprised to see you out here, watching a riding lesson." His dark eyes twinkled as he leaned on the fence railing. "You interested in learning how to ride?"

"Not necessarily."

"You can't live on a ranch and not know how to ride."

"I'll take my chances."

"Tomorrow it's your turn," he promised.

"I wouldn't dream of taking you away from your houseguest," Muriel said, hedging. She wouldn't mind learning how to ride, but she sure wasn't going to do it with an audience of curious cowboys and a smirking Miss Texas.

He winced. "She'll be gone by afternoon. If she isn't, I'll drive her into Dallas myself."

"That bad?"

Ben nodded. "That bad. She's real easy on the eyes, but she ruins everything when she opens her mouth."

Jimmy winked at Muriel, then turned to his boss. "No law that says you have to *talk* to 'em, son. In fact, I thought you didn't like talkin' anyway."

"I don't." Ben sighed and turned to make sure his houseguest was still safely on the placid mare. "But I'm damn fussy what I want to listen to."

He moved away from the railing. "Don't make supper too romantic," he cautioned Muriel. "I don't want her to get any ideas."

"Okay." She tried not to laugh. Every single man watching the voluptuous blonde would have traded places with his boss in a second, and yet Ben Bradley couldn't wait for Miss Texas to leave the ranch.

"SHE SAYS she can't walk," Muriel announced to Ben and Bonnie. They were seated in the dining room, at a table laden with fruit, juices, cinnamon rolls and steaming scrambled eggs under a silver dome. The sausages were still in the oven, waiting for Muriel to put them on a serving platter, and a sliced ham was on the counter.

"Excuse me?" Bonnie Bradley said, looking up from the Sunday newspaper.

"Tessie—Miss Gibbons said she can't walk, not after what Ben did to her yesterday, and she would prefer a tray sent up to her room."

Bonnie turned to her son. "Ben? My goodness. I had no idea this would be such a success, but—"

"I took her riding," he said, ignoring her look of curiosity. "Nothing else. Mel's my witness."

Bonnie turned to Muriel, who edged toward the doorway. "He taught her how to ride."

"She wanted to see the ranch, she wanted to ride but she was afraid of horses and anything else that moves,"

Ben said. He frowned at his mother. "I don't know what you were thinking when you sent her here."

"I thought she was beautiful," Bonnie said. "And a former Miss Texas, to boot. She sounded nice on the phone, like a real lady."

Ben snorted. "Next time send someone I have something in common with."

"I'll fix a tray," Muriel offered. "Would you like me to bring in the rest of the food first?"

"We'll wait," Bonnie said. "Take care of our guest. After all, it's all Ben's fault that she can't get out of bed."

"She enjoyed the ride," Ben lied. He was the one who enjoyed the ride. He'd intended to fix it so that Tessie Mae couldn't wheedle her way into his bed last night, and he'd succeeded. Tessie, with her tight pants and breast-hugging pink shirt, had made her charms clear to every cowboy on the ranch who had walked within sight. Tessie was the kind of girl who would go to the highest bidder.

And he wanted no part of the auction.

Bonnie rose and tossed her napkin onto the table. "Maybe I'd better go check on the girl. After all, she's our guest."

"Good idea," Ben said. He took his empty cup and followed Mel into the kitchen. He helped himself to more coffee, sliced the ham and watched in disgust as Mel fixed a tray. "You shouldn't have the extra work."

"It's my job," she pointed out.

"I'd offer to carry it up to Tessie Mae, but I've spent two days avoiding her bed and I'd hate to screw up now."

"Good idea."

"You want to go riding later?"

"So I'm so sore I can't get out of bed tomorrow morning? No, thanks. I'm up to your tricks."

"I wouldn't do that to you," he promised. "Just a short lesson in the corral. The fresh air would do you good."

"It's ninety-six outside already."

"Wear a hat."

"Why is this so important to you?"

He shrugged. He couldn't explain it himself, except he thought she'd get a kick out of it. "Lori will lend you a pair of boots."

"No rhinestones?"

He chuckled. "Nothing shiny, I promise. Just come riding with me and see the ranch."

She hesitated. "There's something you should—"

"Muriel?" Bonnie stuck her head in the kitchen. "Miss Gibbons would like her breakfast now, if you don't mind."

"It's all set," Mel said.

Ben watched her pick up the tray and leave the kitchen. He liked his housekeeper. She was the kind of woman he could talk to.

If he wanted to talk, of course. Which he didn't. He would teach her to ride and see if she liked it. How could anyone live on the ranch and not know anything about horses?

4

BONNIE OFFERED to take Tessie Mae to the airport. The blonde simpered her goodbyes to her relieved host, who kissed her on her peach-blushed cheek and told her he'd enjoyed meeting her. No one believed him for a minute.

Muriel watched the whole thing while she cleaned up the dining room. Ben escorted the women to Bonnie's convertible, then waved goodbye. The show over, Muriel took the dirty dishes to the kitchen and started piling them into the dishwasher. And to think she'd thought this job would be dull.

"Don't bother with this now," Ben said, entering the kitchen with long strides.

"It's my job," she reminded him. And she liked doing it. It was so different from teaching teenagers that she was actually finding it relaxing. She liked puttering in the kitchen and she liked planning the meals. She liked the view from the windows and she liked having a glass of iced tea while she sat in the shaded screen porch in the afternoons.

"And I'm the boss. Get dressed. There's something special going on you ought to see."

Muriel dropped the sponge in the sink and turned to face her boss. He was a handsome man, that was certain. And he had a certain cowboy charm. Why wasn't he married by now? "What is it? Are you going to make me ride for hours, like you did Tessie Mae?"

He grinned. "She brought it all on herself. She was primping for the boys and she also wanted to see a lot of the ranch. I think she was picturing herself as Mrs. Bradley." He chuckled. "Tessie Mae is a born exhibitionist. Did you get a load of that shirt she had on?"

"It wasn't exactly a shirt," Muriel said. "More like a pink bandage."

Ben chuckled. "Sure had the boys going, though. They'll talk about her for years."

"Speaking of years, it's been that long since I've been on a horse."

"We'll take it slow, I promise."

Muriel hesitated. She was pregnant and she intended to stay that way. She didn't think horseback riding was dangerous, but falling off the horse was the problem. "Will you give me the tamest horse on the ranch?"

"Yep. Angel taught all the kids here how to ride. She especially likes four-year-olds."

"Well, okay." It would be fun to see more of the ranch. Growing up in the city had left her with a lot of fantasies about ranch life. And here she was with an opportunity to see a real Texas cattle operation. "Give me a few minutes to finish up here, then I'll get dressed."

"Come now."

"I can't leave a mess like this."

"Then I'll help." He stepped over to the sink and started rinsing off dishes.

"What's the hurry?"

"Bonnie could decide to come back here," he said. "And I don't intend to be around if she does." He finished loading the dishwasher and shut the door. "I don't want to be late."

"Late for what?"

"You'll see. Something fun."

"As long as I don't end up in bed like your last guest, I'm game."

"Yeah, well, the idea was that Tessie wanted *me* in bed with her."

"And you refused?" Muriel was surprised. A naked Tessie Mae would be a sight to behold.

"Damn right, I did. Tessie looks like she could figure out how to get pregnant and set herself up for a wedding ring. I'm not going to be trapped like that."

Muriel winced. John had used the same word. *Trapped.* Her pregnancy had not been deliberate. She wouldn't have chosen to bring a baby into the world if she'd known she would be raising it alone. Getting pregnant had been a happy accident, not a device to force a man into marriage. "Sometimes a woman can't help getting pregnant," she offered. "It takes two."

"Well," Ben drawled. "I wasn't going to be one of them."

Muriel decided she couldn't picture her boss and the beauty queen together in any kind of intimate way. In fact, she didn't even like *trying* to picture it. "Should I make a lunch?"

"Nope. That's all taken care of."

"I didn't know cowboys were so mysterious."

He winked. "Meet me outside by the big white barn in fifteen minutes. I promise you'll have a good time."

It didn't take her long to change into her baggiest pair of jeans. She could still zip up the zipper, but those days were numbered. Pretty soon she would start to look pregnant and not just chubby. The Bradleys might be a little shocked that their housekeeper was pregnant, but she'd only been hired until October. She'd made it clear she wasn't available after that. In a few weeks they would know why. She really didn't think they'd care, as long as she could still cook and make sure the house was clean. Thank goodness for Lori and her willingness to do the heavy work.

She hurried downstairs and found a pair of well-used boots and a battered cowboy hat on the kitchen table. Ben had remembered. She sat down and finished getting dressed. By the time she left the house and took the path to the barn, she was feeling positively Western. As long as her horse was tame and wouldn't toss her onto the ground, she should be safe. The palomino had looked half-asleep as it walked around with Tessie on her back.

Angel was waiting, standing patiently, tied to the fence railing. She was saddled and ready for a ride, but didn't look too enthusiastic about getting any exercise. Muriel could sympathize.

Ben led his horse out of the barn and came over to them. He dropped the reins, and the dark brown horse stood still.

"Aren't you afraid he'll run away?"

"Baker here is trained." Ben gestured toward Angel's saddle. "You want to get on?"

"I guess so." She put her foot in the stirrup and swung her leg over the saddle. "Those fifth-grade riding lessons are finally going to come in handy."

Ben adjusted the length of the stirrups, then handed her the reins. "Pick up the reins in one hand, then guide her by touching the reins to the side of her neck in whatever direction you want her to go. Take a left? Touch the right side of her neck. Got it?"

"Got it." Muriel smiled. It was a hot afternoon, but there was a breeze. Horses always smelled good, and so did the leather of saddles and reins. Angel still hadn't moved or shown any reaction to the fact that someone was sitting on her back, which was definitely comforting. "Where are we going?"

"It's a surprise," he said, getting on his horse.

"I'm too old for surprises." She gave Angel an experimental nudge with her heels and the horse moved three inches. So far so good. She liked a horse who didn't want to bother causing trouble or doing all that feeling-its-oats kind of baloney.

"Not a surprise for *you*," he said, watching to see that she was following him. Angel walked after the brown horse as if it was her own idea. "A birthday surprise for Jimmy. It's his fiftieth, and the only way Joyce could surprise him was to plan it out at the old homestead. Most of the men will be there to help him celebrate."

"A cowboy party?" She'd never been to something like that before.

"We usually call them barbecues," Ben said, giving her a strange look. "Jimmy thinks he's meeting me there to discuss whether or not to burn the place down."

"Sounds like fun." Muriel started to relax. Angel was on automatic pilot, so all she had to do was stay in the saddle and keep her hat on.

"Yeah, well, it all depended on how fast I could get rid of my guest."

"Weren't you afraid she wouldn't be able to leave at all?"

"Nope. I told my mother to get her out of there."

"Your mother doesn't seem like the kind of woman to take orders." That was an understatement, of course. Bonnie Bradley was sure used to running the show. Muriel wasn't sure if she'd ever met anyone quite like Ben's mother.

"She knew she'd pushed me too far," he said, guiding his horse past the maze of barns and corrals.

"How far are we going?"

"Just a couple of miles."

"Miles?" Her thighs would be screaming for help within the hour.

"You'll be fine."

She wanted to believe him. The sky was blue, the breeze warm, and it felt good to be outside having a life. She felt like she'd been holding her breath for the past months. Keeping secrets wasn't easy. Rearranging her life hadn't been a piece of cake, either. Muriel took a deep breath and exhaled, finally feeling freer than she'd felt since the home pregnancy test had read Positive.

They rode in silence for a while, over slight rises in the landscape, beside a dry creek bed, along a trail between a grove of trees. Muriel was content to hold on to the saddle horn and the soft leather reins and let Angel follow the big brown horse.

She could watch Ben that way. He was every woman's image of a cowboy. His worn jeans fit him quite nicely. His boots were worn and brown, and the light cotton shirt covered a set of wide shoulders. Dark hair curled over the collar of his shirt, and a cowboy hat topped the entire picture. He seemed like a man who was happy with who he was and where he lived. Too bad his mother was determined to change him.

He was a nice guy.

Muriel blinked. She didn't need to be attracted to her boss. She didn't need to be attracted to anyone. She was a pregnant, out-of-work home economics teacher. She was no blond beauty like Tessie Mae. She couldn't fill out a tank top or apply eyeliner like a beauty pageant contestant.

"Mel?"

Muriel looked up. She realized Ben was waiting for her to say something. "What?"

"I asked if you wanted to stop."

"How far away are we?"

"Another ten minutes or so, but we're in no hurry."

"I can keep going," she said, perfectly comfortable. She felt like she could ride across Texas this afternoon. She never felt nauseous in the afternoons, and the fresh air was feeling pretty darn healthy.

"Sure?" He gave her a look. His eyes were shaded by the brim of his hat.

"Yep. But thanks," she added. "I'm okay."

"I really didn't mean to hurt Tessie," he said, holding his horse still. "She exaggerated."

"I'm sure she did." Like she exaggerated those breasts and those eyelashes, too. "She seemed like the type."

He frowned. "Do I look like the kind of man who would want that kind of woman?"

"Am I supposed to answer that?"

"Yeah."

"I don't know you well enough to know what kind of women you're attracted to."

He lifted the reins and moved his horse to stand beside hers. "Not one with fake breasts, I'll tell you that for sure."

Muriel laughed at the expression on his face. "She was a beautiful woman."

"And a real pain in the ass."

"Yes." Muriel grinned. "She was."

"Wonder what my mother will come up with next."

Muriel couldn't imagine. Bonnie Bradley certainly seemed to have strange ideas of who or what was good for her son. "Is it soon?"

"Don't know. I hope the next one is a blonde, too. I like blondes." He nudged his horse to a trot and motioned for Muriel to follow. She brushed her dark curls behind the wide brim of her hat and urged Angel to keep up. It was ridiculous to feel a tiny bit disappointed. She was the housekeeper, the maker of ham sandwiches and a soon-to-be mother. The fact that her handsome boss preferred blondes shouldn't hurt her feelings.

"YOU CAME!" Joyce waved to her as they rode up. Several Jeeps and a couple of motorcycles were parked behind the rickety cabin that nestled in a slight rise of the land. "I'm so glad you could get out here."

Lori hurried up to take her horse while Joyce went over to talk to Ben. "I would've given you a ride, but Ben said you'd rather ride."

"He did?"

The teenager winked at her. "He'd rather be on horseback than anything," she whispered. "Everyone else fights over the motorcycles. I heard Miss Texas left."

"Waddled right out the door," Muriel said, climbing down from the horse. Her thighs trembled a little, but her knees held her up. "I might not be much better tomorrow."

"You'll be fine. Come on, I'll introduce you to the guys."

"Where's your dad?"

Lori looked at her watch. "He'll be along in about half an hour. He's always late."

Ben had dismounted from his horse and touched Muriel's back. "Mel? You okay?"

"Just fine." She tested her balance. "What should I do with Angel?"

"I'll take care of her," Lori offered. "There's a corral behind the cabin."

"Thanks." Ben put his arm around Muriel's shoulders and guided her toward a group of men that were standing by a metal folding table. "You want a beer?"

"Just a soda, thanks."

"Not much of a drinker, are you."

"No." She would drink champagne after the baby was born, though.

The men fell silent as they approached. They tipped their hats and smiled and seemed pleased to meet her. Ben pulled a can of soda out of a bucket of ice and handed it to her. Then he introduced her as "Miss Mel, the new housekeeper at the big house." She knew she would never remember all their names, though she wished she could. Jake, Matt, Shorty, Bob and Oats. She repeated the names to herself. Ben continued to introduce her to people milling around. Crepe paper had been strung around the porch, and tables covered in red checked plastic were laden with food. Mel figured Joyce must have been cooking for a week. She wished she'd known. She could have contributed something to the party.

"Where are you from?" one of the men asked.

"Houston."

The skinny young man waited for her to elaborate, but Mel didn't add anything. "Heard you're a real good cook, ma'am."

"Thank you. You'll have to stop in for cinnamon rolls."

His eyes lit up. "Really?"

"Sure. Now that I'm getting used to things around here, I'm going to start baking."

Ben took her elbow again. "Look." He pointed to a rider approaching from the east. "The guest of honor is about to be surprised."

"Yep." The young man called Oats grinned. "He's gonna be real pi—upset, all right. He hates surprises."

"He just hates turning fifty."

By the time Jimmy cantered up to the group, his face was red. "What in hell is goin' on here?"

"Happy birthday, Daddy," Lori hollered, and the others joined in. Joyce stepped around the horse and gave her husband a kiss. The ranch hands cheered, and someone handed the guest of honor a paper cup full of cold beer. Mel got a kick out of their enthusiasm. They were like one giant family, happy to support each other. Ben had moved away from her in order to shake Jimmy's hand. The older man gave him a good-natured swat on the arm, then jumped from his horse without spilling a drop of his drink.

Clearly the party had begun.

MEL HELPED the Suentes women serve the huge bowls of Mexican food. Several other women, wives of ranch hands who lived on distant parts of the large ranch, had arrived for the festivities. Mel guessed that at least fifty people, plus children, had come to the birthday. Jimmy was the foreman, Joyce had told her proudly. He had been born on the Triple Bar S. "Right here in this cabin. That's why I wanted the party to be here. It's special."

Muriel sliced thick squares of corn bread. "I wish you'd told me about this," she said. "I could have baked something."

"You have enough to do at the main house," Joyce said. "Bonnie is up to something this summer, and I'm glad I'm not in the middle of it."

"She said she's trying to find a wife for her son."

Joyce snorted. "If she cared about him, she'd leave him alone. That boy is fine just the way he is. He's a quiet one. He doesn't need any fancy wife in his life."

"He doesn't seem very quiet to me."

"He's private. And he's happy. Bonnie Bradley should remember her own marriage before she starts trying to get her son in the same position. I heard about that magazine idea. Pure nonsense, if you ask me."

Mel slid the pieces of bread onto a bright orange platter. "Maybe he wants to get married."

"Not to anyone his mother picks out, that's for sure." She took the platter and moved it to one side. "Think I should put the cake out now or wait until later?"

"Wait." Mel looked at the table crowded with food. "I don't know where you would put it."

"Okay." Joyce put her hands on her hips. "I guess we can let them chow down now." She raised her voice. "Come on, you guys. The food's going to get cold!"

She didn't have to say it twice. Mel helped several of the small children fill their plates. Ben had a toddler slung over his shoulders, but he handed him over to his mother for dinner. The child laughed and pulled Ben's hat as he left his perch.

"What about you?" Joyce asked.

"I'll eat in a minute."

Joyce shook her head. "That's not what I meant. What are you doing on the ranch?"

"Working."

The older woman shot her a knowing look. "Running away from something, I'd guess. Something you won't be able to run from much longer." Her gaze dropped to Mel's abdomen, then she winked.

"How did you—"

"A good guess." Joyce moved closer and handed Mel a large spoon. "You want to help serve the refried beans?"

"Sure."

"One thing." The woman's dark eyes were serious. "Are you married?"

"No. Never."

"Is there a man who's looking for you?"

Muriel didn't want to be anything but honest with the woman who could be a friend this summer. And she needed a friend. "No. He's glad I left when I did."

Joyce started to say something, but Ben interrupted. "What's so interesting over here?"

"We're talking about all those women Mel is going to be cooking for this summer."

He put his arm around Joyce's ample waist and squeezed. "You could leave Jimmy and come live with me," he teased. "Save me from all those magazine women who just want my cowboy body."

Joyce shook her head. "You'd better not let Jimmy hear you."

Ben winked at Mel. "I've warned him to treat you right."

Mel laughed as Joyce moved away to rearrange the stack of napkins. "Aren't you going to eat?"

"Yes, ma'am." He picked up a thick paper plate. "I never refuse a meal."

"I've noticed. That's why I have a job." She dumped a serving of beans on his plate, and he scooped some Spanish rice next to it. Trays of enchiladas and tamales lined the table, with big bowls of homemade salsa in between them.

"Where'd you cook before?"

"At home."

He filled his plate but didn't move away. "In Houston."

"That's right."

"Why did my mother hire you if you'd never cooked before?"

"I have a degree in home economics, Ben. Do you want some corn bread?" She didn't mention the teaching degree. That part of her life was over, at least for now.

He gave her a strange look, as if he sensed she didn't want to talk about herself, and took a chunk of bread from the offered platter. "You're entitled to your secrets," he drawled.

"Thanks." Mel smiled at him. "I appreciate that."

Ben didn't mean it. He took his plate, waited while she filled hers and made certain she didn't eat alone. He wouldn't have had to worry. Several of the younger, unattached men crowded around her at the picnic table and attempted to impress her with their wit.

He could have told them they were making fools of themselves, but he didn't. Mel wasn't a flirting woman. She was the solid type, the kind of woman who baked bread and fried bacon and had supper ready on time. She didn't flirt with cowboys or wear pink tops that showed off her nipples, and she didn't look like a woman who would answer an ad in a magazine in order to meet a man.

And he wanted everyone to stay away from her and leave her alone.

Including himself.

BONNIE SAT at her desk and cursed her own stupidity. She'd selected someone she thought had the personality to deal with a shy rancher. And she'd ended up scaring him off.

Stupid girl. Stupid mother, was more like it, Bonnie thought. Well, she'd learned something. Bonnie dumped a stack of envelopes onto the white carpet and prepared to spend her evening coming up with candidate number two.

This was one of those times she could use an assistant, but Bonnie preferred living alone. She preferred finding a daughter-in-law by herself, too. She put on a classical CD, loosened her satin robe and prepared to spend the evening tossing any and all perfumed envelopes into the trash. There would be no more candidates who wafted in Beautiful and wore more makeup than Cindy Crawford. This time she would find a woman who had something in common with Ben. A woman who could share his life.

Bonnie smiled, picked up an envelope and sniffed. Damned if she was going to have to come up with Ritter's bull. She'd rather come up with a wedding.

A wedding that wasn't her own, of course.

THEY RODE HOME side by side in the twilight. Ben was overly cheerful from a couple of extra beers. Mel was worn-out from a day that had begun with eating crackers and fighting the need to bend over the toilet. She clung to the saddle horn and ignored the reins. Angel knew her way around the ranch much better than her rider, and besides, the horse showed no inclination other than walking beside Ben's horse, matching the gelding's leisurely pace.

"You okay?" Ben's low voice broke into Mel's sleepy thoughts of her comfortable bed and her plans for her day off tomorrow.

"I'm fine." To her surprise, she really was. Although tomorrow might be a different story. "That was a great party."

"Yeah. Joyce can sure cook."

"She's going to teach me how to make tamales."

Ben didn't say anything to that, so they rode in silence for a few more minutes while Mel mentally ran over her list of things to do in town tomorrow. She'd called the only obstetrician in Rose River. Fortunately he was accepting new patients. If she liked him, she'd have her records transferred from Houston. She decided not to worry about what she'd do if she didn't like him. Go into Dallas, she guessed, though the ninety-minute drive didn't appeal to her in the least.

"Feel free to ride Angel whenever you want," Ben said. "She could use the exercise."

"Thanks, but I don't know how to saddle a horse."

"One of the boys would do it for you. Someone's usually around, or have Lori show you." He cleared his throat. "Is she working out okay?"

"Just fine. Why?"

"Just wondering." Just trying to make conversation, he added silently. Riding through the semidarkness with a woman by his side seemed to require that he talk. But Mel didn't seem to mind riding along in silence. He glanced over at her a few times. Once she yawned, but she didn't look unhappy. They were back at the barn faster than he would have wanted. He helped her dismount, telling himself he was simply acting like a gentleman, but he sure didn't mind holding her for one brief moment.

Just because he didn't want to get married didn't mean that he didn't like the feel of a woman in his arms.

"Thanks," Mel said, wobbling a little as he released her. His hands automatically went to her shoulders to steady her.

"You okay?"

She looked at him, and he couldn't resist dipping his head and touching his mouth to those sweet-looking lips of hers. It was as if he'd forgotten that she was his cook. It was as if every thought had flown from his mind except that the fragile warmth of her body under his clumsy hands made him want to wrap her in his arms.

Which he didn't. He moved his lips across hers and she lifted her chin a fraction as if she wanted to kiss him back. Her lips were soft as she returned the kiss for a brief second. Ben pulled her closer to him. A normal reaction to sweet kisses in the dark shadow of a barn, but Mel resisted.

She looked at him with those dark eyes, and he wished she'd take those glasses off so he could see her expression. She didn't look scared, but she didn't look as if she wanted to stay and kiss, either.

"Sorry," he said, hoping that would keep her from running away.

"Me, too," she whispered, stepping away from him. She turned and left him with only the two horses for company. He watched as she hurried down the path. He waited until he saw the kitchen lights go on before he turned to the animals.

"No bigger fool than a man who's had too much beer," he told Baker. The horse shook his head, as if reminding his owner that he was tired of standing there watching Ben try to kiss the cook.

5

"TOMORROW IS my day off," she wrote. "Will take the station wagon and go to town. Need some groceries for the week. Casserole in the fridge for supper and plenty of ham for sandwiches." Mel left the piece of paper by the coffeepot before she went to bed. She didn't want Ben expecting eggs and bacon tomorrow morning. Tomorrow she could stay in bed and, in a horizontal position, eat crackers until the sickness passed. Now *there* was something to look forward to.

Mel took a quick shower, admired the slight bulge of her abdomen in the privacy of the bathroom and eventually climbed into bed. Not until then did she let herself think of the kiss. She couldn't believe she had stood there and kissed him back. Just stood there beside her horse and lifted her lips to his. Dumb.

Stupid. Idiotic. And so embarrassing. She'd just been kissed by one of the most handsome men she'd ever seen. Those dark eyebrows and charcoal eyes and those high cheekbones had combined to make her lose her senses.

And here she thought she'd learned better than that.

Mel rolled onto her side and pulled the cotton sheet over her shoulders. The air-conditioning kept the house cool and comfortable, no matter the temperatures outside. It had gotten a little hot out by the barn tonight. She was so glad she had a day off tomorrow. One whole day to avoid Ben and pretend they hadn't kissed. One whole day to figure out how to act when she saw him next.

Which would be the day after tomorrow, if she was lucky. Maybe Tuesday she could fry his eggs without remembering he'd kissed her.

BEN DIDN'T MEAN to follow her. He got a glimpse of pink dress and brown curls from the side of the house as he headed for his truck.

He hoped she wasn't mad about the kiss. He wondered where she was going on her day off. So he picked up the pace and corralled her in the driveway. "Hey," he said, catching up with her. She turned, and he caught the surprise and dismay in those brown eyes. Even the glasses couldn't hide the fact that she wasn't happy to see him.

"Oh, hi."

"Aw, hell," he muttered. "You mad?"

Mel shook her head. "Not at you."

"You should be," he volunteered. He tried out a smile, just to see if he could make her smile back.

"No." She did smile. Sort of. "It's okay." She backed up a step, the car keys in her hand. She wore lipstick and had a purse over her shoulder.

"Going to town?"

"Yes."

"Dallas or Rose River?"

"Rose River."

"So am I," he lied. He'd actually planned to drive north, along the western border of the ranch, to check on the herd summering out there. There were other things he needed to do, like paperwork in his office, but he liked to be outdoors. Cows were always a good excuse.

"I have a lot of errands to do," she said, sounding mysterious again. He wondered if she had a boyfriend, if there was some man looking for. He wondered why she'd moved to a place like Rose River. He thought maybe he should start finding out.

"Yeah. So do I. I could drop you off somewhere and meet you later."

"It's my day off. If you don't mind, I'd just rather go by myself. I wouldn't want to hold you up while I was shopping."

"Sure." He pretended to understand. "I just thought, with the tornado warning and all, you'd rather not be alone."

Her eyes widened. "Tornado warning?"

"Sure." He was a shameless lying scoundrel. Which suited him just fine. "I keep the weather channel on all the time in the med barn. There've been warnings." He took advantage of her hesitation and touched her elbow, guiding her toward the truck. "I won't get in your way," he promised. "You just tell me how much time you need and where I should pick you up."

Mel climbed into the truck and put her purse on her lap. "Just drop me off anywhere downtown, I've got some errands that will take a while. Is there a library?"

"Yes, ma'am. Right on the edge of town, across the street from the hospital and the newspaper office."

She fastened her seat belt as he guided the truck out of the driveway. "We're not in any hurry."

Meaning she thought he drove too fast. Ben eased the pressure on the gas pedal and hoped that would make her happy. He had kissed her last night, he intended to do it again, and he didn't want to make her angry in between.

He dropped her off in the middle of town. He gave her directions to the bank, one block from Main Street, and pointed out the JCPenney's while she stepped out of the truck. He thought about asking her if she wanted to meet at the Pastime Café for lunch, but decided to save his breath. She looked like a woman who wanted to shop. He tipped his hat and she gave him a little wave once she stepped onto the sidewalk.

"Four o'clock?"

Mel looked at her watch and nodded, so Ben drove off down the street in hopes of finding a parking space. He'd stop in at the bank, then pick up a few things at the hardware store. Obviously he wasn't going to get much time with Mel. She would spend all afternoon doing her mysterious female errands, and he could go back to the ranch and take his pick of about fifty chores until it was time to come back to town and get her. He looked into his rearview mirror and caught a glimpse of someone in a pink dress crossing the street toward the bank. It was almost noon already. He wished he'd asked her to have lunch with him at the café. He hated to eat alone.

THE HEARTBEAT POUNDED loudly through the room, and Mel smiled with pleasure. She'd heard the baby's heartbeat once before, but the thrill was still the same as the first time.

"You and your baby seem to be doing just fine, Ms. Madison." The doctor removed the equipment, stripped off his gloves and picked up his chart. "Why don't you get dressed and meet me in my office? I can answer any questions you have, and we'll go over the basics."

"Thank you." Mel waited for the doctor to leave the examining room before she put her clothes on. Getting in to see him today had been a stroke of luck. When she'd gone to the office to see if she could get an appointment, a friendly receptionist asked her if she was free in fifteen minutes. The woman with the twelve-thirty appointment had given birth to a boy last night.

It had taken almost that long to fill out the forms, Mel realized, even with a copy of her records from Houston. One waiting room wall held a bulletin board covered with pictures of babies. Clearly Dr. Connelly was a very busy man. Younger than she'd expected, he'd explained he'd settled in Rose River recently so his wife could be close to her family. Mel thought that was sweet.

She sat across from Dr. Connelly's desk while he perused her chart. "We have an excellent hospital here," he said. "It's small, but well equipped. When you get a little farther along, there are birthing classes you can attend. I see that you're not married."

"No."

"You might want to consider giving some thought to selecting a birthing coach. That can be anyone you trust. Mother, sister, significant other. I'd encourage the Lamaze method of natural childbirth, but we can discuss other alternatives as we get closer to the due date." He looked at the papers again. "October twelfth, I see." He looked up and smiled. "A Saturday during college football season, Ms. Madison. That's not very good planning on your part."

Mel returned the smile. "I'll see if I can hurry things along a day or two."

"I'd appreciate it. I'm a big A&M fan and I hate to miss a game." He grinned, to show he was teasing, then stood up. "Irene will give you a packet of information about the hospital and the birthing room," he said. "There's a sample of vitamins, too. You're taking vitamins already, I hope?"

"Yes."

"Eat well, try to avoid sweets and fats, get some exercise but don't overdo it. Sexual intercourse is permissible right through the nine months. Use common sense and try to get enough rest. Any questions?"

"When does the morning sickness stop?"

"You're at twenty-one weeks, I see. You should have stopped by now, but some women are sick longer. It shouldn't continue much longer, and your blood tests, according to your records, came out fine. Have you lost weight?"

"No. I think I've put on about nine pounds, but I'm not even in maternity clothes yet."

"Have you had an ultrasound done?"

"No." Christine had them done with her three children. She'd been able to see her baby on a screen and take home a picture. "But I'd like to."

"Fine." He scribbled something on a pad of paper, then handed her the form. "You can have it done at the hospital. If you're lucky you might even get in today, but you'll probably have to make an appointment for next week. I'm sure everything is fine, though."

"Thank you." She tucked the form into her purse.

"I don't usually recommend amniocentesis unless there's something in the family history that warrants the procedure, and I don't see anything here that makes me think it should be done." Dr. Connelly shook her hand. "Call me anytime if you have any questions. Make an appointment for next month. We'll see you once a month until September, then we'll start every other week, then once a week until the baby is born."

Mel slung her purse over her shoulder. She thanked him once again, and as he followed her out into the hall he reminded her of her promise not to go into labor during a football game. Mel turned the corner to the waiting room just as a tall cowboy opened the door and peered inside. Two very pregnant women looked up at him and smiled. They thought Ben was somebody's husband, Mel realized. He had that worried look on his face.

It was too late to go back into the hallway. He'd spotted her and started across the room. Then his steps slowed as he realized he'd walked into a female domain. He removed his hat. "Mel?"

Mel crossed the waiting room quickly. "What are you doing here?" She tried to keep her voice down.

"I was worried. I was driving out of town when I saw you come into the clinic. I waited outside in the parking lot for a hell of a long time and then I started to think you were sick." He looked around at the pictures of babies and the stacks of *Parents* magazines on the table. "I went into three other doctors' offices looking for you. What the hell is this place?"

"Out. Now," Mel whispered. "Get out of here. I'll meet you—"

"Ms. Madison!" The receptionist leaned over the counter and waved. "You're forgetting your gift pack! You don't want to miss out on the free offers or the coupons for Pampers, now, do you?"

Mel hurried over to the counter, took the thick bundle and through gritted teeth thanked Irene for the information.

"No problem!" She gave Ben a cheerful wave. "You and Mr. Madison have a nice day!" When Ben stared at her, she winked. "This is your first, isn't it?"

"First what?"

The two pregnant women laughed. Mel took Ben's arm and pushed him toward the door. "Out," she repeated. "You've got no business being in here."

"I was worried," he repeated. "You can't blame a man for that." They stood outside on the sidewalk. He put his hat on and Mel blinked against the bright sun. The sky was as blue as it could be, with a few fluffy clouds clinging to the horizon.

"There's no tornado, is there?"

"East of here," he insisted. "Those damn things can travel fast."

"You were spying on me."

"I didn't mean to." He looked at her. "First *what?*"

"None of your business."

His gaze flickered to the packet she clutched to her chest. "*Joys of Childbirth?*"

Mel lifted her chin and stared at him. He was going to have to know sooner or later. She'd be showing soon, and there was no way to keep it a secret. She would have preferred to wait a few weeks, though, until she'd proved herself to be a competent enough housekeeper to keep her job. "I'm having a baby."

Confusion clouded those gray eyes. "Why?"

"Why?" she repeated. "Why do you think?"

He took her elbow. "Come on. Have you eaten?"

"No, I'm not—"

"I am," he said, leading her across the street to a wooden building with neon letters announcing that it was the Pastime Café. "We'll talk there."

"Maybe I don't want to talk," she grumbled. "Maybe I want to shop at JCPenney's."

"Yeah, and maybe I want to have a hamburger with my pregnant housekeeper." He hustled her through the door, found a private booth near the back wall and thanked the waitress for the menus at the same time he pushed them aside.

"Now," he said, leaning forward. "You want to explain this?"

"No."

Her simple denial seemed to stun him. "No?"

"It's none of your business," Mel felt it necessary to point out. Aside from her doctors, she'd discussed her pregnancy with two people, her sister and her boyfriend. Ex-boyfriend. She didn't intend to discuss it with anyone else.

"Wrong," Ben drawled. "You're working for me. I have a right to know."

"I don't think so. Not as long as I can do the job you hired me to do."

"For how long?"

"I agreed to work until the first of October."

"And when is the baby due?"

"October twelfth."

He frowned and leaned back as the waitress set glasses of ice water in front of them. "Cutting it a little close, aren't you?"

"As long as I'm healthy, it shouldn't make any difference."

The waitress picked up her pad. "You folks ready to order?"

Ben looked at Mel. "What do you want?"

"A vanilla milk shake and a hamburger with lettuce and tomato, please." She might as well enjoy someone else's cooking for a change. Then she could go to JCPenney's and find some more sundresses and maybe a pair of pants with an elastic waist. And a couple of baggy T-shirts, too. She didn't realize that Ben had ordered, the waitress had left and that her boss was waiting for her to say something. "What?"

"I asked if you're feeling all right."

"I'm fine."

He didn't look convinced. "The doctor said so?"

"Yes."

"Is there a husband somewhere who's going to come after you?"

"No." Mel took a sip of water and opened her packet. In spite of everything that had happened, it was exciting to think that she was going to have a baby. Here in Rose River. With Dr. Connelly, who certainly seemed nice. If she could just ignore Ben and his infernal frown.

"Does the father know?"

Mel looked up from a fascinating flier on breastfeeding. "I'm going to say this once more. My personal life is none of your business. As long as your house is clean and your meals are on time, you should be happy." His eyes narrowed. He didn't look happy at all. She wondered if he'd fathered any children he didn't want and then decided Ben wasn't the kind to turn his back on a woman in trouble.

Still, you never knew about men. Mel turned to the breastfeeding article, then leafed through the rest of the pamphlets. There was nothing in there about raising a child all alone. There were no articles on how to cope with single motherhood and men who refused to admit they'd fathered a child. Still, she would manage. She was going to have a baby. A baby she wanted very much, no matter how difficult the situation was. She would survive, and she would be fine doing it by herself.

Something fluttered in her abdomen. Mel held very still and waited. It happened again, the tiniest movement inside of her. The papers dropped from her fingers to the table and she looked at Ben. He was watching her with worried eyes. "The baby just moved."

"Just now?" He leaned across the table. "Is that good?"

"Yes." She giggled and put her hand on the tight bulge beneath her waist. "It stopped." She looked at the cowboy, whose features had relaxed. "It stopped. Darn." She shook her head in wonder. "I've read about it, and knew it should be happening soon. And I heard the heartbeat again today. They let me listen in the doctor's office."

Ben didn't say anything, but he stared at her as if she had gone crazy. Mel realized she'd made a mistake. Her excitement overshadowed everything else, and she forgot that she needed to keep her personal life private. Blithering on about the details of her pregnancy was not going to help her keep her job. "Sorry." She lifted her hands from her abdomen and smoothed her skirt. "I shouldn't have—"

"No," Ben said. "It's okay, but—"

"Here you go, folks. Two burgers, one deluxe and one deluxe with fries." She set the thick plates on the table. "I'll be right back with your milk shake. Anything else?"

"Coffee," Ben said.

Mel shook her head. "I'm all set, thanks." She put catsup on the burger and discovered after the first bite that she was hungry after all.

"WHY IN HELL haven't you returned my calls?"

Bonnie opened the door of her apartment wider and motioned for her son to enter. "Come in, dear. And stop bellowing."

"Two weeks," he roared. "I've been calling you for two weeks, and what do I get? Nothing but the answering machine. Where the hell have you been?"

"Away."

Lord save him from mysterious females. "Away," he repeated. "Fine. You were *away*. I need some information."

Bonnie smiled and patted him on the arm. "Come," she said. "Let's sit down. You haven't been to the city in the longest time, I can't quite believe my eyes. Would you like a drink? I have an appointment in an hour, but we still have time for—"

"No drink. I want—"

"To know about the next woman I've selected, of course." Bonnie went over to her desk and riffled through some papers until she found what she was looking for. "Here. Her name is Candy. And you have a lot in common."

Ben ignored the paper his mother tried to hand him, so she dropped it on the glass-topped table between them. "I'm not here to find out about the next magazine woman, Mother. I'm here because—"

"Why not? She's arriving on Friday, and she sounds adorable. I've spoken to her on the phone. And I've seen her picture, too. But I'm not going to show it to you. You'll just have to be pleasantly surprised."

"Yeah. If Tessie was any example, I'm going to be ready to hang myself by Sunday afternoon. You'll have to forgive me for not getting real excited."

"Stop sulking and sit down." Bonnie sat on the opposite sofa and crossed her legs. "Now, tell me what you're doing in Dallas. Tomorrow is the Fourth of July. I thought you and the boys would be getting ready to celebrate."

He ignored the question. "I came about Mel."

"Mel who?"

"Muriel. Madison. The housekeeper you hired. I want her résumé."

Bonnie stood and went back to the tiny corner desk. She sat on a spindly chair and opened a drawer. It only took her a few moments to locate the sheet of paper. "Let's see," she said, returning to the couch. "What do you want to know?"

"I'll take that." Ben held out his hand and his mother leaned forward and handed him a sheet of cream stationery.

"I should have put it with the employee files, but I haven't had time. What on earth is the matter with you?"

He scanned the information. It didn't tell him much. Just that she'd worked for the Houston School District for seven years as a home economics teacher. It gave her birth date, education, address and phone number. References included her high school principal and the owner of a bakery. He didn't know what he had expected. A sentence naming the father of her baby? He folded the paper and tucked it into his shirt pocket. "Anything else you can tell me about her, like why did you hire a woman you didn't know?"

Bonnie shrugged. "She had wonderful recommendations. It's not easy to find good help these days."

"Did you know she's going to have a baby?"

His mother turned pale. "Ben, you haven't—"

"It's not mine," he insisted. "I'm not in the habit of sleeping with the hired help."

Bonnie closed her eyes for a moment, as if saying a prayer of thanks. Then she looked at Ben and tilted her head. "So what exactly is the problem? She's only temporary."

"Maybe." For some weird reason, he couldn't picture Mel leaving the ranch. The vision of Mel, baby in her arms and suitcases at her feet, didn't make any sense. In fact, it irritated him.

"Definitely. She made that quite clear when I hired her." Bonnie glanced at her watch. "I'm running late, darling. Was there anything else?"

"Other than the fact that the housekeeper's pregnant and you're saddling me with another crazy houseguest?

I guess not." He stood up and clamped his hat on his head. "I'll be heading home now."

"Try to stay under eighty. The state police are getting cranky."

"I'll keep that in mind." Ben headed for the door, but stopped before he opened it when Bonnie called to him.

"Have a lovely weekend. I'll be down to meet the young lady, of course."

Ben glared at her. "It's a good thing King Midas is worth all this. You sure you can deliver?"

Bonnie gulped, a fact that her son didn't overlook. "Mind your manners, entertain the women, and we'll see what happens."

"A bet is a bet," he reminded her. "Ritter had better be ready to sell that bull to the Triple Bar S."

"We'll see. *After* you meet Candy Corbin."

Ben opened the door and, once out in the hall, slammed it with a satisfying bang. He'd spent two weeks trying to find out more about Mel and all he got was a piece of paper listing a bunch of stuff about her previous job. He already knew she'd been a teacher.

He drove home fuming. He wanted to know what bastard had done this to Mel. He wanted to plant his fist in the middle of the guy's face and he wanted Mel to be all right. She wouldn't talk to him about anything. She'd been baking like it was Christmas, though. Trying to distract him with cinnamon rolls had worked for a while, until he'd caught on. And he was getting tired of tripping over cowboys who just "happened by" the kitchen and ended up leaving with cinnamon rolls or a handful of oatmeal cookies.

Back there in Rose River, in the café, when she'd felt her baby move for the first time, she'd looked almost pretty. Her eyes had glowed with happiness, and she'd smiled as if she'd been given a Christmas present. He'd been stunned and, damn it, attracted to her. Just like he had been that night after Jimmy's birthday party.

Well, he'd have to entertain Candy Somebody. Maybe that was a good thing, after all. Maybe he'd get over worrying about Mel for a few days.

"HE'S SO SWEET," Lori continued. "But because he's a Ritter Dad's real reluctant to let him hang around."

Mel draped a clean dish towel over the bowl of dough and set it on the counter. "What's a Ritter?"

Lori squeezed the mop, then dipped it in the soapy water before continuing to wash the tiled floor. "The owners of the ranch next door. Something happened years ago, something between Ben's father and Old Man Ritter. Jack's the youngest son, just a year older than me. One of those late-in-life surprises, I think. His mother died about ten years ago, and he lives with his dad."

"How many Ritters are there?"

"Two older sons, one who works in Dallas and another in Galveston. Neither one wants anything to do with the ranch. Except Jack, and his father thinks he's too young to know anything about anything."

Mel sat down in one of the kitchen chairs. Lately all she'd wanted to do was sleep. The minute two o'clock came, it was as if all of her systems shut down. Mel yawned behind her hand, leaving a smudge of flour on her nose. She had on one of her new dresses today, a lavender print of tiny flowers on a white background, but it was covered with the huge white apron she liked to wear in the kitchen.

"Are you all right?" The teenager tossed her dark braid behind her and picked up the mop. "I can do something else if you want to go lie down."

"I'm fine. Just a little sleepy." She hadn't told the girl she was pregnant, but she had a feeling Lori's mother had.

"I cleaned the guest bedroom. Gave it a dusting and clean sheets, and put some daisies in a vase on the table." Lori hesitated. "Are you sure you don't want me to do anything else?"

"I'm sure." Mel smiled and hid another yawn. The sleepiness would pass, or she would take an hour and lie down in her room. It was a quiet time of day, but there was still supper to prepare. Ben was having company again. And if this one was anything like Tessie Mae, then they were all in for one long weekend.

"Damn it," Ben said, striding into the kitchen. He went to the sink, grabbed a glass from the overhead cupboard and poured himself a drink of cold water. He was wearing his usual denim outfit, and the perspiration on his forehead did little to detract from his usual good looks. He swiped his forehead with his arm, drank the rest of the water and turned around to look at the two women. "We've got company."

"She's here?"

"Yeah. I saw her coming up the road. With a horse trailer."

"She brought her own horse?"

"Either that or she's planning on taking one of mine home with her." He set the glass on the counter. "Doorbell's going to ring any second."

It did, as if right on cue.

Lori laughed. "You want me to answer it?"

"No," Mel said, getting to her feet. "You're off duty. I'll do it."

"I'll do it," Ben offered, moving away from the sink.

"I think you'd better wash up before you meet her."
Mel untied her apron and tossed it over a chair as she left
the kitchen. "You smell like a horse."

"What else am I supposed to smell like?" she heard him
grumble, but he went down the hall to the bathroom
while she went toward the foyer. It only took a second
to open the front door, and there stood Annie Oakley
reincarnated as a big, healthy blonde. She was easily five
foot ten, even without the snakeskin boots. She was
dressed in buttery yellow suede, and a thick yellow braid
hung over her shoulder. Her skin was tanned, her eyes
blue and lively, and she looked as if she could wrestle
steers to the ground in the rodeo.

"Hey, there!" The young woman reached out and
shook Mel's hand until Mel thought her fingers would
cramp. "Nice to meet you. Am I in the right place? Is this
the Triple Bar S, home of the Texas cowboy who's looking to settle down with the right woman?"

Mel opened her mouth, but no sound came out. It
didn't seem to bother the new houseguest. She tossed her
leather backpack over her shoulder and brushed past
Mel to stand in the foyer.

"I'm Candy Corbin," she said, looking around the
foyer. She peeked into the living room. "Nice place he has
here. You have any beer? I could use a cold one."

"Sure. I'm Mel, the housekeeper. Why don't you make
yourself comfortable in the living room and I'll tell, uh,
Mr. Bradley that you've arrived."

"Yes, ma'am. Don't forget the beer, either, okay? It was
a hot drive. And would you know where I could put my
horse? He's not real happy 'bout being cooped up. I'd
sure like to get him settled, and Ms. Bradley said there'd
be plenty of room for him."

"I'd be glad to." Mel hurried into the kitchen and caught Lori as she was leaving. "She has a horse," she told the girl. "Should she put it somewhere?"

"I'll have Dad take care of it," Lori offered, keeping her voice low. "I peeked at her. She's really something, isn't she? Like from a rodeo."

"I know what you mean."

"Think Ben will like her?"

"I would think so. She seems more of his type than Tessie Mae."

"Where'd he go? He should be—"

"Oh, my Lord, you're a big, handsome one, aren't you?" Candy cried. Her booming voice could clearly be heard from the living room.

Mel grinned. "I think Ben just met his date for the weekend, don't you?"

6

BEN HURRIED to wash up in the downstairs bathroom. He scrubbed the Texas dust from his face and dried his hands on the clean towel Mel had supplied. He frowned. Was she working too hard? He didn't know much about pregnant women, but he sure as hell didn't want anything to happen to Mel or her baby. Anyone who worked for him was like family. It had always been that way on the Triple Bar S, and it wasn't going to change just because of a few houseguests making trouble.

When he glanced into the mirror, he thought he looked presentable. He couldn't help smelling like a horse, but he didn't give a good gol-dam about how he smelled. Any woman who stepped foot on his ranch couldn't— shouldn't—be too fussy about what smelled and what didn't. Any woman on the Triple Bar S knew she'd be visiting a rancher, not a stockbroker with manicured fingernails. Ben hurried to the living room and stopped short.

A yellow-haired woman stood with her hands on leather-covered hips and gave him a big grin. She was almost as tall as he was, and almost as dusty. She crossed the room in swift strides and held out her hand. "Oh, my Lord, you're a big, handsome one, aren't you?"

"Hello," Ben said. "You must be Candy Corbin." His hand, taken in a powerful grasp, squeezed hers briefly. But the smiling square-jawed woman made no move to release him.

"Damn right," she bellowed, giving him a wink. Her eyes were blue, her face freckled, and she wore no makeup. The healthy giant with a sparkle in her eye was holding him captive. Ben gave a little tug, and the woman reluctantly released his hand. "I've come all the way from Austin to meet you. And no way in hell am I disappointed!"

Ben backed up a step. He gestured toward one of the sofas. "Would you like to sit down?"

"Hell, no." She chuckled. "But I will anyway, just to make you happy. I'll be damned if I can figure out why a man like you has to put an ad in *Texas Men* magazine. You'd think the women around here would have jumped your bones before now."

"I see you brought a horse trailer with you," Ben began. He sure as hell didn't want to discuss bone-jumping with a strange woman. Or with any woman, for that matter.

"Yes, sir. Brought my prize mare, Grand Lady Anne. Sired by Sir Ashley Downes, champion quarter horse. Know him?" Ben nodded. He thought he'd heard the name. "I call her Grandy. Can't get into that three-name shit."

Candy and Grandy. All right. "Would you like a drink?"

"That little housekeeper of yours said she'd get me a beer."

Ben stood and went over to the bar. Nothing would do but whiskey. He poured himself a generous portion and took a quick gulp.

"You a drinker?"

"No."

"Too bad." Candy grinned. "I like a man who knows how to have a good time."

"Not me," Ben insisted, swallowing the next mouthful slower than he would have liked. "I'm not much fun." Mel entered the living room. She carried a large tray, which she set down on the coffee table. "Am I, Mel?"

"Are you what?"

Clearly Mel hadn't been listening. "Fun," he repeated. She gave him an odd look, then poured beer into a glass for his houseguest.

"Depends what you mean by fun, I guess." She took a platter of cheese and crackers from the tray and offered a snack to his guest. "We won't be eating supper until seven. Just let me know when you'd like me to show you to your room, all right?"

"Thank you kindly, Miss Mel, but I think Ben here can show me just about anything I need to see. Maybe more." She gave him a wink and bit into a piece of cheese.

Ben turned to his housekeeper. He wished she didn't look so damned remote. She'd taken off that apron and wore a pretty light purple dress. He'd noticed she liked dresses. They hid her pregnancy, so he guessed that was the reason she wore them. He hoped she wasn't hiding it for his sake. Maybe she was still shy about the whole thing. "I'll, uh, show Candy her room after she finishes her drink."

"Okay, boss. Whatever you say." Mel turned away but not before Ben saw her try to hide a smile. So she thought his predicament was funny, huh? She wasn't going to be laughing as the weekend wore on. He was certain Candy's voice boomed throughout the house, so Mel would get an earful by Sunday afternoon.

"Ben? Hey, honey, you daydreaming?" Candy waved a finger and pointed to the cheese tray. "Come sit down beside me and get something to eat. You look like you could use some refreshment."

"Well..." He stalled, but he didn't want to be rude. "All right." Ben sat on the opposite end of the couch and took another gulp of whiskey. Candy Corbin looked as if she enjoyed sex at gunpoint. With her hand holding the gun, of course.

His mother had fixed him up with a overheated version of Annie Oakley.

He hoped he'd survive the weekend.

"LORI, GO HOME. I really don't need your help." Mel put the finishing touches on the platter of cold sliced beef. The sprigs of parsley added much-needed color.

The teenager continued to unload the dishwasher. "Do I have to go? I want to see what happens next."

"Nothing's going to happen next," Mel fibbed. "I'll serve supper to them, then after dessert I'm going to bed."

"Do you think they will?"

"Together? I doubt it."

"Why not? I thought men liked aggressive women."

Mel shook her head. "You've been reading too many magazines, my girl. Men like to do the chasing. Most of them don't like to feel like they're being hunted down like dogs. But I could be wrong. Ben could be the kind of guy who needs a woman to come after him."

Candy's loud laughter echoed from the dining room.

"At least someone out there is having a good time," Lori said. "I don't know. He looks a little edgy to me. Like he'd rather be somewhere else."

"Yes, he certainly does." It was that trapped expression. She remembered it well from her other life. On another man's face. Her hand went to her abdomen and touched her growing belly.

"Is the baby moving?"

"No. Not now." Mel opened a jar of smoked oysters. "Ben might need these tonight," she muttered, a little aggravated by the vision of Ben in Candy's bed. That woman looked as if she could rope and hog-tie Ben if he didn't come willingly.

"Do you feel it often?"

"Usually when I'm lying down. It's more of a flutter than anything else." She arranged the oysters in a serving dish, then reached into the refrigerator for the pasta salads she had prepared earlier. The temperature had hit ninety-seven today, but the house was still fairly comfortable. The air-conditioning was a blessing, but Mel liked to avoid heating up the kitchen in the afternoons.

"I'll bet you can't wait."

"Sometimes," Mel admitted. "But sometimes I think I can wait until October to be a mother."

"Like I can wait till August to be a college student?" Lori grinned.

"Something like that." She handed the girl a bowl of potato salad made with fresh chives and cottage cheese. "Would you put that in the dining room?"

"Sure."

Mel busied herself with taking the plastic wrap from the other dishes. She didn't want to talk about her pregnancy with an impressionable teenager. She didn't want Lori to think that being a single mother was something glamorous. It was pretty darn scary, if anyone really wanted to know. What if this was a boy and he hated her for not having a husband? What would her daughter do without a father to teach her how to dance?

"Miss Mel?"

Mel looked up to see Lori staring at her. "What?"

The girl smiled. "You were a million miles away. I asked if you want me to put everything on the table now."

"Yes. I'll tell Ben that he can feed his guest now." Mel didn't bother untying her apron before heading toward the living room.

"Dinner's ready," she said. The couple looked very cozy on the couch. Candy still wore her leather outfit, but she'd kicked off her boots and was curled up on the leather sofa looking as if she owned the ranch already.

Ben looked a little stunned. Mel noticed he held an empty glass in his hand, which he set on the table before he stood up. "Thanks, Mel. You're joining us, aren't you?"

It was a plea for help, since they usually ate together in the kitchen. "Of course not," she said, wondering if Candy's lips looked as if she'd been kissed recently.

"Join us," Candy said. "The more the merrier!"

"Thanks, but no." Mel motioned toward the dining room. "Everything's all set. I hope you enjoy it."

Ben shot her an anxious look. "You'll be around?"

"Just call when you're ready for dessert."

He grumbled something under his breath.

"I could eat a goddamned stuffed pig and come back for seconds," Candy declared, standing up. "I worked up an appetite this morning. Barrel-racing practice, you know. Makes a woman raring to go for the rest of the day."

"I'm not at all surprised," Ben said. He pointed her toward the dining room. "Just go right on in there. Sit anywhere your little ol' heart desires."

OYSTERS. He didn't think that was funny, though Candy gave him a wink when she helped herself to some and then passed him the dish. Mel had a sense of humor, that's for sure. Though he didn't much care for being the butt of it.

He set the damn things aside and helped himself to beef. Mel had a way of spicing it up and serving it cold that made his mouth water.

His houseguest had piled her plate high with everything offered. She'd asked for another beer. Which made five, not that he was counting. He watched her when he figured she wasn't looking. Candy Corbin could sure demolish a plate of food, all right. He wondered if all her appetites were as large and felt himself shrivel.

He didn't want to take her to bed. That wasn't part of the invitation, though maybe some women would figure it was. Come to think of it, Tessie Mae had given him the distinct green light.

"What's wrong? Off your feed?"

"No." Ben managed to look pleasant. Candy rested an elbow on the table and munched on a roll.

"My daddy used to say there ain't much paw and beller to a cowboy. He could've been talking about you, all right. You're a quiet one."

"Yeah. Guess so."

"Miss Mel is one hell of a cook. The baby yours?"

"What?"

Candy blinked her big blue eyes and grinned. "Can't hold it against you. A big strapping man like yourself must get a little lonely out here. Well..." She leaned closer and put one large hand on his thigh. "Your lonely nights could be over, cowboy."

"It's, uh, not my baby." He pushed his chair back and escaped her touch. He didn't want her to get any higher and think he was the first Texas eunuch or something. "Want another beer?"

"Sure. What the hell. I'm not driving tonight." She reached for the oyster dish and emptied it onto her plate. "Want to get some more of those oysters, too, while you're up?"

"Yeah." He took the dish and pretended not to understand the eager look in her eyes. "I'll ask Miss Mel."

"Hurry back, handsome. I get lonesome in fancy dining halls like this one."

Ben took his time walking to the kitchen. He wished he could keep right on walking, down the hall and outside and on to the barn. He'd saddle up one of the horses and spend the rest of the weekend out under the stars. He wouldn't let anyone find him, either. He'd hide. Hide from Candy and Bonnie and even Mel. Especially Mel, who wouldn't tell him anything about herself or the baby's father or what she was going to do come October, when she turned into a mother.

It was driving him crazy.

Mel was still puttering in the kitchen. He slammed the dish on the counter with more force than he'd intended and he felt bad when Mel jumped a little. "Oysters?" he roared, then tried to keep his voice down. He'd bet Candy had ears like a cat. "You think that's funny, don't you?"

Mel didn't look at him. She was busy frosting something that looked pretty damn good. "I thought it might be necessary, considering the eagerness of your guest."

"Well, she can be as eager as she wants. I'm not playing."

"No?"

"No, damn it. You can't leave me alone with her."

Mel finally looked at him. "I think you can take care of yourself, defend your own honor, so to speak."

"She doesn't want my honor, *so to speak*."

"I still think you can handle it." Mel smiled at him. Ben had an overwhelming urge to take her into his arms, but she held a knife in her hand. It didn't look sharp, though. He took a step closer and touched her cheek.

"Mel," he began, but she stepped away from his touch. A flicker of surprise crossed her face before she turned back to the cake.

"Chocolate," she said. "I heard it was your favorite."

"Yeah." He cleared his throat. "Thanks."

"No problem."

"We're riding tomorrow. Come with us."

Mel shook her head. "Horseback riding is too risky, and I don't think Candy would want to keep it to a walk, do you?"

"I don't care what she wants. Just go with us."

Mel finished frosting the cake and scraped the excess frosting off the knife with her index finger. Before she could lick it, he reached out and took her hand. He nibbled the frosting with his lips, tasting the sweetness of chocolate and the fascinating texture of Mel's skin against his tongue.

"Ben—" she began, but he didn't let her pull her hand away.

"I'm not finished," he said, licking once more. He released her and she stood there looking at him.

"I wish you hadn't done that."

"Why?"

She moved toward the sink, turned on the water and washed her hands. "I would think it's obvious."

"You mean because I have a date in the dining room and you're pregnant with another man's child?"

"Yes," she said, turning to him. "I think that about covers it."

She didn't have to be sarcastic. He resisted kissing her. He told himself she'd probably hit him if he did. Either that or she'd sink into him the way she did that night by the corral. Hell. He was in a bind either way.

He took a step backward. "Have a picnic ready for tomorrow afternoon. Make sure it serves three." Ben stomped off, pleased he'd gotten the last word in. That wasn't easy to do when you were talking to women.

He returned to the table. Candy was busy helping herself to another load of beef.

"Thought you were getting more oysters," she said, her gaze drifting to his crotch. Ben sat down in a hurry.

"We're out." He picked up his fork and looked at his unfinished dinner. He wished he was eating frosting instead.

"Are we riding early tomorrow?" She gave him an arch look. "Or are we sleeping late?"

Ben pretended he didn't understand her meaning. "I've got an appointment with a sick cow in the morning. Thought we'd go riding at eleven, take a picnic lunch, show you the ranch."

"Good. Grandy can use the exercise, and so can I."

He pushed his plate aside. He'd lost his appetite. He wondered if Mel was still out there in the kitchen. "You want dessert?"

"Sure." Candy demolished the rest of her beef and wiped her mouth with the napkin. "You sure have one hell of a cook."

"We'll eat out on the porch," Ben said. "I'll tell Mel to put the coffee on."

Candy stood, picked up the dirty plates and followed him across the hall and into the kitchen.

"You don't have to do that," Ben said. "You're a guest."

"A guest who picks up after herself," Candy said, putting the dishes by the sink. "Want me to wash them up real quick?"

"No, it's okay." Ben picked up the note by the coffee-pot and read it. "Mel's gone outside for a while. She left us coffee and cake." The plates and dessert forks were displayed by the two-layer cake. Candy came up beside him.

"Chocolate. My favorite."

"Yeah." Ben could still taste Mel's skin on his tongue. "Mine, too."

MEL LIKED HER. The big woman might be crazy about Ben and have a mouth that needed to be washed out with soap, but Candy Corbin had a kind heart. She poured her own coffee and she wasn't allergic to the words *thank you*. She loved her horse and anyone else's horse. She liked the ranch. She was in her element when it came to sunshine and dust. No tight-fitting pink shirt for Candy. She wore denim and leather and well-worn boots. Earlier this morning she'd performed part of a trick-riding exhibition for Ben and Jimmy. Mel had seen Joyce and Lori walking toward the large corral to join the crowd.

The ranch hands were in awe once again, though Mel was beginning to suspect it didn't take much to impress them. This latest houseguest was a Texas Amazon, and she walked like she had holsters strapped to her hips.

But she was not Ben Bradley's type. Mel wasn't quite sure she knew what type Ben deserved, but the cowgirl wasn't it. Ben's mother had come closer this time, but Ben had stayed in his own bed.

Mel, to her great disgust, had checked the sheets this morning. She'd told herself it was a Saturday laundry chore, but she knew she was lying to herself and to Ben when she'd met him on the stairs.

"I didn't sleep with her," he'd said. "As if that was any of your business." Still, he'd grinned at her when he'd said it, and she'd felt like a fool.

"I'm the housekeeper, not your chaperone." She'd sniffed and continued down the stairs. But her heart was lighter, and she'd started whistling "The Yellow Rose of Texas." Which made no sense, but she'd been in the kitchen ever since, whipping up sweet dough and packing containers for the picnic.

"Pack enough for a crowd," Ben said, entering the kitchen with Candy close behind. "We can hitch up the horses and take the old wagon. Lori volunteered to take the reins. What do you want to do?"

"The wagon sounds fine," Mel said. She didn't bother to argue about going. It was a beautiful day, cooler than yesterday. "You can ride your horses then, right?"

"Yep," Candy answered for him as she slapped the dust off her jeans. "Any coffee left?"

"Half a pot. I'll get—"

"Don't bother. I sure as hell can't stand to be waited on. Gives me the goddamn creeps."

Mel tried not to laugh as she pulled a mug from the cupboard and handed it to the woman. "By all means. Help yourself."

Ben sprawled in a kitchen chair and tipped his hat from his forehead. He looked content to watch Mel fix the picnic supplies. Candy joined him, scooting her chair closer to him than it had been.

"Have you met my mother?" he asked her.

"Nope. Never had the pleasure."

Mel turned around and caught Ben's expression. He looked like a man trying to figure out a puzzle.

"Did you talk to her on the phone? I mean," he drawled, his voice casual, "how did she invite you to the ranch?"

Mel had been wondering the same thing. Surely Mrs. Bradley wouldn't have considered the outspoken Candy as a daughter-in-law. She removed the platter of beef from the refrigerator as quietly as possible and waited to hear the answer.

"Damnedest thing," Candy replied. "I wrote that letter weeks and weeks ago, while I was recovering from a nasty ankle sprain. Your mother called when I was on the road barrel-racing. We never could reach each other on that damned phone. She left messages with my answering service. I left messages on her machine. Finally she just left a message for me to show up here, if that was convenient. Hell, I figured you were only six hours from the Davidson rodeo, so what the hell. I'd seen your picture." She winked at Ben. "You were worth the drivin' time."

"Thanks."

Mel turned away to start slicing bread. Ben liked her homemade wheat bread for his sandwiches.

"Too bad you're so skittish," Candy muttered, trying to whisper. "We've already wasted one night."

Mel didn't turn around, but she raised her voice. "Miss Corbin, do you like mustard or mayonnaise on your roast beef sandwiches?"

"Thought I told you to call me Candy," she grumbled. "Mustard. And lots of it, too, if you don't mind."

"No trouble at all." Mel sneaked a peek over her shoulder at Ben. He had that trapped expression again. She almost felt sorry for him. "Mustard for you, too, right, boss?"

He didn't answer.

"Mustard," she repeated, knowing he was having his own troubles. "Right?"

"Yeah. Sure."

"Hey," Candy said, giving him an elbow. "We've got something else in common!"

LORI'S YOUNG MAN met them on the trail miles from the main house, near a creek where cottonwood trees gathered in a clump of shade. Ben greeted him kindly, and Lori brought the wagon to a stop and made the introductions to the ladies.

Jack Ritter was a handsome young man with an engaging smile and friendly green eyes. And he only had eyes for Lori.

"Sure you don't mind my joining you, sir?"

"No, Jack," Ben told him for the third time. "Whatever went on between our fathers has nothing to do with us, that's my feeling."

Jack went back to making cow eyes at Lori while Ben dismounted and walked over to the wagon to give Mel a hand getting down. She wore jeans today, and they looked new. A long shirt covered her belly, but he could see the swell of the baby there. Did it move a lot now? He wondered if he could ask.

"I'm okay. Thanks." Mel released his hand and reached for the boxes in the back.

"I'll get those," he said, sounding gruffer than he'd wanted.

"Thanks."

"You okay?"

"Sure." She turned those brown eyes on him. Her glasses had slipped down the bridge of her nose, so she pushed them in place. "Why wouldn't I be?"

"You're starting to show," he pointed out. "Maybe you shouldn't work so hard."

She smiled at him and he felt his heart flip in his chest. "This isn't exactly the most strenuous job in the world, Ben. But thanks for asking." She started to move away, but he put a hand on her arm.

"The baby—" He hesitated. "Does it move a lot, like it did in the café that day?"

Her face lit up. "Yes. More and more. Especially at night."

"At night," he echoed, feeling a shocking stab of longing to be in bed beside her. He knew her skin would be warm and she would smell like cinnamon.

Mel blushed as if she could read his thoughts.

"Mel, I—"

A gunshot rang out over the prairie, making them both jump. Lori screamed and Mel crumpled to the ground. Ben turned in the direction of the sound. What in the hell had happened now?

"SHE DIDN'T MEAN anything," Mel said once again. She'd been repeating the same words since yesterday. Candy had apologized, and Mel felt like an idiot for fainting. She never fainted. She'd never heard a gunshot so close, either. "She was just trying to protect the horses, I think."

"That snake was nowhere near the horses. She was trying to show off and scared the hell out of all of us," Ben grumbled. "I didn't even know the damn rifle was loaded. I sure didn't expect her to whip it out and kill a rattler."

"She has incredible reflexes."

"Yeah. You could have been hurt."

"I'm fine, and I think she feels bad about the whole thing," Mel pointed out. It was Sunday morning, the cinnamon rolls were fresh out of the oven with the white frosting drizzled on top in an enticing pattern, and the coffee was hot and black. Considering all that, she expected Ben to be in a better mood.

He took another sip of coffee. "I had to lock my bedroom door last night."

"Poor baby."

"I'm serious, Mel. I think she'd hurt me. Probably ride me so hard my private parts would fall off."

Bonnie stuck her head in the kitchen. "Now that's a disgusting picture," she drawled. She didn't look too pleased with her son. "I take it this date didn't go well, either?"

"Come on in, Mother. If you're lucky, Candy will come in shortly and you can meet her."

"I'm looking forward to it." She sat down at the table. She was dressed in a pale ivory pantsuit that must have cost a small fortune, and her golden hair was in her usual smooth bob. But she looked tired, as if she'd been awake half the night. Mel put a mug of coffee in front of her and she automatically reached for it. "Thank you, dear."

Ben eyed her from across the table. "I showed her a good time. Romantic dinner, horseback riding and a picnic. Right, Mel?"

"Right. He's been a perfect gentleman. Would you like a cinnamon roll?"

"No. I'd rather meet Miss Corbin."

Ben pointed out the window. "Then head out to the main corral. She's putting her horse through its paces right now. She likes exercise and she likes being outdoors."

"Which should have been a match made in heaven." Her eyebrows rose. "What's wrong with this one, besides your fear of losing certain parts of your anatomy that are going to waste anyway?"

"Go meet her." Ben smiled an evil smile. "See for yourself."

THE THREE OF THEM waved goodbye as Candy guided her truck and trailer down the driveway. She'd left with no hard feelings, she'd said, though she'd given Ben one last longing look before she'd climbed into her truck.

"A standing invitation, Ben, honey," she'd said, waving at him. Mel had given her a thermos of coffee and wrapped some cinnamon rolls in tinfoil so she'd have a snack for the long ride home.

"Yeah," he'd said, about as noncommittal as a man could get.

"I don't know what I'm doing wrong," Bonnie muttered as she shaded her eyes and watched the truck and trailer disappear down the road. "There were hundreds of letters. Hundreds," she repeated. "I must be missing something."

Ben put a comforting arm around her shoulder. "You can't pick out a woman for me from a bunch of letters. Now, how much does Ritter want—"

"I'm not done," she snapped, and Mel scooted into the kitchen while they argued in the foyer.

She left them alone and enjoyed having the kitchen to herself. She'd fried eggs this morning without feeling queasy, so things were looking up. Those elastic-waist denim pants had come in handy this weekend, and she'd have to buy some of that odd-looking maternity underwear at JCPenney's tomorrow. And a new bra. Her breasts had expanded to overflow her normally tiny bras. She felt positively busty for the first time in her life. Too bad her belly was growing almost at the same rate.

RITTER LIKED the black lace teddy, so Bonnie made sure she wore it Monday afternoon when he appeared at her apartment. He'd had a meeting at the bank, and she'd agreed to give him lunch. They both knew that "lunch" had nothing to do with food.

"Bonnie, sweetheart," Ritter murmured, slipping the straps from her shoulders. "When are we gonna make this legal?"

"Don't," she murmured. His hands stopped. "Not that," she said. "Don't start *talking*."

"Hell, Bonnie." He kissed the swell of her breasts above the lace. "I ask you to marry me every damn time I get your clothes off. Think you'd be used to it by now Think you'd give up and say yes."

She stripped off his shirt in record time, with experienced fingers. She knew Ritter's body almost as well as her own, but she'd be damned if she'd marry him. "I hate being married. You know that."

"I ain't Clay, honey." He slid in bed and patted the empty space beside him. "Come on in here and I'll prove it."

Bonnie slipped underneath the sheet and snuggled against Ritter's solid warmth. He was built like a bull stocky and low to the ground, and she loved him dearly "You don't have to prove anything," she whispered. "You know that."

"I know you need a man in your life," he grumbled pulling her toward him.

"Ben runs the ranch," she countered, wriggling against him. "And you—well, you know what you do."

"Stud service," he whispered. "And I'm a hell of a lot cheaper than King Midas."

"Sell him to me."

"He's yours," Ritter promised, fitting himself inside of her. Bonnie reached up for him and smoothed her hands on his shoulders. "Everything I have is yours if you marry me, darlin'."

She moved against him, deliberately making him forget to talk. She was a foolish woman who'd made a bet she couldn't keep. Bonnie closed her eyes and let her man love her.

7

"I'LL RAISE YOU two," Jimmy said, tossing the chips into the pile in the center of the table. He studied his cards again, as if unwilling to believe he held a good hand.

"I'll see you two and raise one," Ben said, tossing three chips toward the pot. The others passed and threw down their cards, so Jimmy showed his hand. A pair of aces and a pair of tens.

"Three queens," Ben crowed, and scooped the pot toward him. A pile of chips already waited there to be sorted into piles. "You're not having much luck tonight are you, boys?"

"No." Jimmy gazed morosely at his bottle of beer "Guess it's not my night."

A heavyset man on Ben's right chuckled. "What's tha they say, Ben? Lucky at cards, unlucky at love?"

The others laughed while Ben took his time shuffling "Yeah. Well, I'm not lucky in love so I'd better have some kind of luck beating you at cards."

"Unlucky," another man said, guffawing. "Big hand some bachelor like you has women traipsing through the ranch all the time. I don't call that too unlucky."

"Ante up," Ben said. "You saw the last woman?"

"Heard about her. Champion barrel racer, wasn she?"

Ben dealt the cards. "Yeah. And she liked shooting rattlers."

"Sounds like a handy woman to have around," another man commented.

Ben shrugged.

Jimmy picked up his cards and frowned. "She was better than that first one, you got to admit."

Oats looked up over his cards. "You talking about the one with the big—"

Mel entered the living room with another tray of homemade pizza sliced into squares. She set it down on a small table next to the poker table. This was her first poker night, and she got a kick out of the way the men took it so seriously.

"Smile," Oats finished.

"Here you go," she said, dropping a stack of paper napkins on the table. "That should take care of you for a while, okay?"

Six men smiled at her. Six sets of eyes darted to her belly and back to her face again. She'd started wearing maternity clothes on Monday, when she'd gone to town—without Ben this time, thank goodness—and raided the small mothers-to-be section at JCPenney's. She was six months along now, and it was getting harder to be discreet, though the basic sundresses on sale in the misses section served as great maternity clothes, too. She was growing a little tired of tiny-flowered prints, that was all.

"Thank you kindly, Miss Mel," one of the men said. She couldn't remember his name, but he'd been at the birthday party.

"Yes, ma'am," the others agreed, while Ben frowned at her.

"Don't carry any more of those heavy trays," he said. "I told you that you didn't have to wait on us."

"It wasn't that hea—"

"Just don't do it again," he grumbled.

Mel's eyebrows rose as she stared at him. He'd been grumpy since Candy left, grumpy since his mother had come and gone, grumpy for the past three days. She planned to avoid him for the rest of the week and hoped he'd have cows to chase in another county. She turned away from him and looked at the other men, who all wore identical amused expressions. "There's the salami Jimmy brought fixed on a platter with cheese and roast beef, and I fixed a big platter of nachos. Let me know when you're ready for that and I'll heat it up."

She left the room and Ben threw down his cards. "Count me out of this one," he muttered, and followed Mel to the kitchen.

"What's the matter with you?" she asked, opening a can of soda.

"I've won seventeen dollars so far," he said.

Mel fixed herself a tall glass of ginger ale and took a sip. "Winning at cards makes you rude, too?"

"What do you mean?"

"You've been like an old bear since Candy was here," Mel said, turning to face him. She put her hands on her hips, and he thought she looked cute, with her glasses sliding down her little nose like that. She pushed them into place and glared at him. "What on earth is the matter with you?"

"You could have been hurt."

"The tray wasn't heavy, you big—"

"I'm not talking about the tray," he said, raising his voice. "You could have been hurt when you fainted like that!"

Mel looked surprised. "That was days ago, and I talked to my doctor. He didn't seem concerned. He said it happens sometimes. Pregnant women can be more sensitive to—"

"Gunshots," Ben finished for her.

"Surprises," she corrected. "It was pretty embarrassing, and I wish you'd just forget it happened."

Ben deliberately put his large hand on the mound made by Mel's growing child. His long fingers spread wide enough to almost encompass the swelling.

"Forget it happened," he repeated, with an entirely different meaning. He stared at her, into those brown eyes that held no clue to what she was thinking or feeling as he touched her so intimately. "Is that what you're in the habit of doing? Forgetting?"

"Yes," she snapped, but she didn't move. She looked at his hand, then to his face. "As much as I can, considering."

"I'll hunt him down for you, if you want."

"I don't want him," she said, her voice pure steel. "I want the baby. *My* baby."

Ben understood. The man had rejected her, refused to live up to his word, and Mel had too much pride to force him. She would go her own way, of course. With her child.

Who kicked him. And made him draw his hand back in shock. "What the hell—"

Mel smiled. "She's just saying hello. It was just a little nudge, actually."

His palm burned, so he rubbed it on his thigh. He felt a little dizzy himself. Ben Bradley, the man who had delivered an uncountable number of calves. "She?"

"Just a guess."

He bent his head and touched his lips to hers. Once again it was an immediate jolt to the rest of his body, touching her like that. He kissed her hard, he kissed her soft. Her arms twined around his neck and her breasts touched his chest and he was on fire with wanting her. She parted her lips, and he touched her tongue with his, and they kissed for long moments, swift seconds, he didn't know. He lifted his mouth from hers, just a little, just enough to look into those dark eyes and check if there was fear or passion in their depths. Passion, he thought.

"What—" she began, but he stopped her.

"Just a kiss," he said, taking possession of her mouth again. He lied, he knew. He wanted more than a kiss. He wanted to carry her into a bedroom, any room, and make love to her. He wanted to touch those soft breasts and fit himself inside her body and he wanted to make love to her as tenderly and completely as he knew how.

Ben backed away, released her and, trying to hide how shaken up he was, left the room. He was a lust-crazed maniac who should be locked up in the Rose River jail.

Mel blamed it all on hormones. Not that Ben wasn't a good-looking man with a way of kissing that made her heart threaten to stop pumping blood. And not that he didn't have a certain appeal, being protective and kind and all that. And not because she'd developed a fondness for the smell of leather and dust or because he made her laugh with his teasing, either.

None of that counted, after all. Because she was six months pregnant with another man's child. She shouldn't feel sexy, but she did. She shouldn't want to feel Ben's hands on her breasts, but she did. She wanted to curl into him and enjoy every sweet sensation her body could muster.

She'd never felt better. One morning she'd woken with no queasy feeling, and the next minute she'd been counting yeast packets and making more sweet dough than she could knead in one lump.

It was hormones. Had to be. The little devils were coursing through her bloodstream and messing with her brain. She wasn't a sexy woman. Never had been the kind to attract men just by walking into a room. Nondescript brown hair, nondescript brown eyes, plain old plain face on top of a plain old plain body. She couldn't even wear her contact lenses—they'd bothered her since the pregnancy.

She'd never lacked for dates, though, because most men enjoyed someone ordinary, someone not intimidating. Someone who was like everyone's sister.

And now she was pregnant, feeling ripe and sweet as a good melon, and she should lock herself in her room.

She really should.

THEY TRIED to avoid each other for more than a week. She cooked his eggs and burned his bacon, and Ben said thank you and then worked outside for the rest of the day. He ate his lunch outside and his supper in the dining room, while he read the paper and Mel puttered in the kitchen. She preferred to eat later, in the cooler hour after sunset. She told herself being around Ben wasn't good for her digestion.

Mel took her day off and went to Rose River. She drank a vanilla milk shake in the Pastime Café, received a reassuring pat on the back from Dr. Connelly and saw her baby on the ultrasound equipment at the Rose River hospital. The technician even printed a picture, which Mel kept in her top dresser drawer. There was no decision as to whether the baby was a boy or a girl, though the technician offered to make a guess.

She even found a shop that specialized in maternity clothes and bought some nicer-looking underwear and a cotton nightdress that actually had room to spare. She still wasn't that big, though the doctor assured her that some women just carried their babies differently. She was gaining the right amount of weight and doing fine.

She was doing fine until the following week, until she served roast beef again.

"Save the scraps," Ben said.

"Okay." She gave him an odd look. He'd never asked her to save scraps before. In fact, he hadn't ever told her to save anything. "Why?"

"Hasn't Lori shown you the puppies?"

"No." Lori was the busiest teenager in the state of Texas. Last week she'd been to initiation at the university, and she was busy buying clothes, working her other jobs and sneaking off to see Jack Ritter whenever she could find the time.

"Come on, then," Ben said, scraping his uneaten beef into a bowl. He took a knife and cut it up into small pieces. "They're old enough for this now."

Mel untied her apron and followed him outdoors. He'd been later than usual for supper. The sun was already setting, and there was a peaceful quiet that settled over the ranch in the evenings. She followed Ben along the wide path to the outer barns. Joyce, taking her laundry off the line, waved. Mel waved back, but Ben didn't stop. He led her into the enormous old barn and whistled.

A shaggy brown-and-white spaniel peeked around one of the posts, then ran out to greet her master. She wagged her tail and whined when she smelled the meat.

"You've seen Ranger around, haven't you?"

"Yes." Mel bent to pat the dog. "From a distance. We've never been officially introduced." The dog wagged her tail, then turned her attention to the tall rancher.

"Come on. Ranger's been busy. She hasn't left the barn too often." He led her down the wide center aisle of the barn to a back stall, smaller than the others they passed. Five brown-and-white puppies, the image of their mother, tumbled through the mounds of straw to greet their mother and see who could be the first to sniff Ben's boots.

"Oh." Mel breathed, unable to resist. "They're adorable." She sat down on a mound of clean straw in the corner and lifted one curious puppy onto her lap. He looked up at her with chocolate-colored eyes and wagged his tail.

Ben scraped the beef into an old pie plate for the puppies and their mother. Mel released her puppy and watched him scramble to the dish to get his share of supper. Ben sat down beside her. Too close, she thought, but then again, he was still inches away. Maybe just being together in one room was being too close. She felt warm.

"She's really Jimmy's dog," Ben said. "Follows him around most of the time. She likes to ride in his truck."

Mel wasn't really listening. She was inhaling the warm scent of his skin. He'd washed up before dinner, and she could still smell soap and the faintest aroma of his after-dinner coffee. She knew she should get up and go get her kitchen cleaned up, but she didn't move. She told herself it was fun to watch the puppies demolish the pieces of beef and then tumble together around their patient mother's legs.

"Want one? Jimmy'll be trying to find homes for them in a few weeks."

"No." She couldn't imagine anything she needed less than a puppy. "I think I'm going to have enough to take care of pretty soon."

"Every kid needs a dog."

"Maybe someday. Not now."

"You don't have to leave, you know. You can stay, put a crib in your room."

"I can't," Mel said, although the thought had occurred to her more than once. It wasn't right to stay here, to try to work and take care of an infant. She was trying to avoid working after she had the baby, after all. That was the point of the whole summer.

"But what are you going to do?"

"I'll have enough money to take at least a year off, maybe more if I'm careful. I'll live near my sister and eventually, when the baby is older, find another teaching job. Or at least do some substitute teaching for a while."

"You sound like you have it pretty well figured out."

"I have to." She turned to look at him. His face was even darker from the sun now, and those gray eyes were completely unreadable. He reached out one sun-browned hand and cupped her face.

"You all right?"

She nodded. Or tried to. His face was very close, and those familiar lips were brushing against hers in the most wonderful way. It seemed natural to lean back into the straw, which was already piled like pillows behind her. Ben went with her, kissing her completely and taking her breath away. Mel didn't stop to think that she shouldn't wrap her arms around his neck or touch his hair or tug him closer to her. His mouth slanted neatly over hers. His hand found the swell of her right breast and fondled its weight.

She could have melted. It was heaven to be touched. She could almost hear her hormones squeal with pleasure.

"I don't want to hurt you," Ben said, his voice hoarse as he lifted his mouth from hers.

It hurts to stop, she wanted to protest. But he didn't
have any intention of stopping, obviously, because he
turned her gently on her side to face him, and he took her
in his arms and kept on kissing her. His left hand unfas-
tened the row of buttons between her breasts, then he slid
one warm palm across her breast. He eased the sleeve of
her dress lower, then the strap of her brassiere, until an
ample amount of breast was exposed. Ben moved his lips
lower, to tickle her neck and set fire to the skin above her
collarbone. He found the top of her breast and eased the
lace-trimmed fabric lower.

She wondered if they were going to make love right
there in the barn. He had half of the top of her dress off.
There were more buttons, and if he kept unbuttoning
she'd be left in her underwear, and she'd bet he was pretty
good at removing underwear.

"Ben?" she said.

"Mmm?"

"Are we crazy?"

He lifted his head, but he didn't look surprised by her
question. "Why?"

"Because," she said, but his lips had found her very
sensitive nipple, and the sensation was causing her brain
cells to freeze up and die. "This *is* crazy," she said, but
she sighed as he unclasped the center snap of her bra.

"Yeah. I know."

He didn't sound too upset about it.

Mel spoke again. "But—"

"Damn it," he said, moving away from her.

She tried to hide her disappointment. And her relief.
Speaking of crazy, she was obviously someone on the
edge. She tugged the two sections of her dress together,
and Ben turned to her with regret in his eyes.

"There was a goddamn dog licking my neck," he said.

"Probably a good thing, don't you think?"

His gaze flickered lower, to where her hands held the fabric against her bare breasts. "No, I don't think it was a good thing," he growled. A brown-faced puppy peered over Ben's shoulder, making Mel smile despite her embarrassment. "What's so funny?"

"Someone else wants to know what we're doing in here."

Ben scooped up the puppy and leaned over to put him closer to his mother and his siblings. He stood up and brushed the straw off his clothes, then after Mel had fastened her clothes properly, he gave her his hand and helped her to her feet.

"Stay in the kitchen from now on, Miss Mel," Ben said. "Or we'll both do something we regret." With that, he picked up his hat, slammed it on his head and left the barn without a backward look.

Mel played with the puppies for a few minutes, hoping her face would stop burning with embarrassment and ... lust. Hormones, damn it, were complicating her life more than she ever could have expected.

"HE'S NOT HERE." Mel concentrated on fluting the edge of her piecrust. She'd promised Joyce she'd contribute something to the Rose River bake sale. They were raising money to refurbish the old town hall. Baking helped her keep her mind off Ben and where he was and what he was doing and who he was doing it with. She'd already made two pies and had decided to keep on making pies until she was tired of peaches and piecrust.

Bonnie sat at the kitchen table and moved her chair away from any lingering particles of flour. "What do you mean, not here?"

Mel finished the piecrust and turned to Ben's mother. The woman was stunning, dressed in a white pantsuit edged with gold braid. She had the body of someone half her age, and Mel envied the woman her slender waist. She wondered if Ben had found a woman with a tiny waist in Dallas. "He left yesterday morning, before I was up. He also left a note saying he was going to Dallas or maybe Austin and no one was to worry."

Bonnie frowned. "That's strange," she muttered. "It doesn't make sense."

Mel shrugged and went to the next mound of pie dough. "You know him better than I do," she said, picking up the rolling pin. If Ben Bradley walked in here right now, at least she'd have a weapon. He'd left her in that barn, and she hadn't seen him since. The coward. He'd almost made love to her. And she'd enjoyed it, too, darn it all. She supposed she owed that puppy a big favor. There was still part of a roast in the refrigerator. She could cut it up and—

"Mel?"

Mel looked over at Bonnie. "I'm sorry. You were saying?"

"Are you feeling all right, dear?" Bonnie looked worried. "Is the job too much for you in your condition? We can get you more help, I'm sure, or perhaps—"

"I'm perfectly fine," Mel assured her. "I tend to daydream, I guess." About a handsome rancher who unbuttoned her dress two days ago.

"Which is understandable." Bonnie's gaze dropped to the bulge under Mel's apron. "You're still quite small. When is the baby due?"

"October twelfth."

"You have some time to go then." Bonnie sighed. "Benjamin was two weeks late. I thought he'd never arrive. I was a mess. I could barely move. Clay had to—" She shook her head. "Anyway, Ben drove me crazy then and he's still doing it."

It was probably a hobby of his. Driving women crazy, that is. Mel rolled out a perfect circle, then lifted it into the waiting pie plate.

"What kind?"

"Peach. For the bake sale in town."

"What am I doing wrong, Mel? Was Candy really that bad?"

Mel gave up trying to work. The pie dough could wait a while longer, and the sliced peaches were soaking in lemon juice. She fixed two tall glasses of iced tea and brought them to the table. Then she sat down, which actually felt better than she expected it to.

"Thank you," Bonnie said, taking a sip. "This is lovely." She looked at Mel and waited. "Tell me about his reaction to these women."

"Tessie Mae was afraid of horses," Mel said, choosing her words carefully. "She wasn't exactly the ranch type."

Bonnie frowned. "But Candy was. So what went wrong?"

"I liked Candy, Mrs. Bradley."

"Call me Bonnie."

"Bonnie. Candy was a good-hearted person, but she was a little too forward and a little too—" Mel searched for the right word, but gave up.

"Crude?"

"A little, but she was lots of fun. I don't think Ben appreciated her shooting the rattlesnake the way she did."

"I've never known Benjamin to be squeamish about rattlers or guns." Bonnie frowned. "Though he *is* picky about women. Which is the trouble. I thought he needed help with his . . . love life. I want him happy. I want him married, with children. He's the kind of man who needs a family, and yet he holes up on this ranch and talks to the cattle. He could live in town and live off the oil money and date all the Texas debs, but he insists he was meant to be a rancher and that's what he'll be."

"If he's happy—" Mel began, but then stopped. This was none of her business, though talking about Ben was more fun than making peach pies.

"He doesn't know what happy is," Bonnie complained. "That damn son of mine wouldn't know happiness if it hit him on the head."

With a rolling pin, Mel added silently, wondering when she'd developed this violent streak. Ben hadn't looked happy in the barn, either, come to think of it.

"He has some strange ideas," Bonnie continued, tapping her long fingernails on the wooden tabletop. "The next woman I send out here has to be perfect. Absolutely perfect, or none of us is going to be happy." She looked out the window toward the barn and frowned. "Least of all me."

BEN WAS MISERABLE. He'd tried drinking, but the bars were too loud and too raucous. He'd tried calling old friends, but two were out of town and the other three were married. They invited him to dinner to meet the wife and kids. Ben refused. He hoped he'd been polite about it, but women and children were exactly what he didn't need this week.

He needed guy stuff. And plenty of it. His suite at the Paramount was everything a man on the run could hope for, with its own bar, spacious living room, a bed wide enough for an orgy and a balcony that overlooked the city. A balcony he could throw himself over if he got any more lonesome. He hated being lonely. He was better off at the ranch, where there was always someone to talk to. And Mel had cinnamon rolls waiting for him when he came in for coffee in the middle of the morning.

Ben poured himself a whiskey. He wasn't here to think about Mel. He wasn't in the middle of Dallas to think about his warm and desirable housekeeper. He didn't want to think about how he'd suddenly found pregnant women sexy, but on the elevator yesterday.... Well, he wasn't going to think about his reaction to that woman in the pink dress who looked like she was going to calve any day.

He could call one of his father's cronies and see if there was a poker game anywhere, though he was pretty sure Clay played for higher stakes than the guys on the Triple Bar S. Or he could head down to the bar and hope that a beautiful woman would walk in, sit down next to him and offer to fulfill his every fantasy. Of course, she'd have her price. And he didn't do hookers.

Ben picked up the remote control and started checking out channels. There should be a game on. He could order a steak from room service and pretend he was having a good time running away from home.

Running away from his housekeeper was closer to the truth.

He sat on the bed, found a baseball game and wondered if he'd have more fun if he went to Austin instead.

MEL DECIDED she was going to go stark raving mad. With Ben gone, there wasn't enough to do to keep her busy in the kitchen. Bonnie had moved in two days ago and shut herself in Ben's office with a bulging plastic garbage bag and a bottle of Jack Daniels. Every once in a while she came out and refilled the ice bucket.

Lori was no help. The girl alternated between mooning about Jack Ritter and obsessing over her choice of college courses. Mel made sure that Lori cleaned Bonnie's bedroom—though the woman didn't use it much—and taught her how to make cinnamon rolls. Cinnamon rolls were Jack's favorite, too.

Mel wanted to keep busy. It kept her from thinking about her future, about the baby, leaving the ranch, and about almost making love to Ben in the barn. She visited the puppies, befriended Ranger, and contented herself with petting horses and watching Lori train a young gelding who didn't particularly want to be trained. Mel also cooked and froze casseroles in disposable foil containers and stacked them neatly in the freezer for the time when Ben didn't have a housekeeper. No matter what Bonnie said or did, Ben Bradley was a man who was going to stay on his ranch, by himself, on his own terms.

She didn't think those terms included marriage.

Or, she told herself in an honest moment, she hoped they didn't, no matter how hard Bonnie Bradley tried to arrange things. Ben deserved to be happy, and if that meant he wanted to stay single and hang out with the cattle, then he should.

"I'VE GOT IT," Bonnie announced, striding into the kitchen with a piece of paper in her hand. Her blond hair was disheveled, her makeup nonexistent, and there were dark circles under her blue eyes. "I think this is it."

"Is what, Bonnie?" Mel stopped making sandwiches and stared. Bonnie wore a pair of old jeans and a dirty shirt that looked like the one Ben had left in his office last week. She wondered if insanity ran in the family.

"Is what, darlin'?" a male voice asked. Both women turned as a tall, well-dressed older version of Ben stepped through the sliding door that faced the pool. "What are you up to now?"

Bonnie stiffened. "None of your business, you old son of a gun."

The man's eyes darted to Mel and he grinned, then removed his black cowboy hat. "Hello, darlin'. I'm Clay Bradley, and it's a pleasure to meet you."

"Ben's father?"

"Yes, ma'am, and proud to say so, too." He came closer and held out his hand, so Mel took it. He had skin like leather and definite gray eyes. He was a handsome man, just like his son. They were built the same, with wide shoulders and slim hips and long legs. "And you are?"

Bonnie answered. "Mel Madison. The new housekeeper."

Clay's gaze dropped to Mel's belly, then back to Bonnie. "How new?"

"Not that new," Bonnie said. "Although your son is off sowing wild oats in Dallas, I think. Maybe he's following in your footsteps, after all."

Clay didn't blink an eye. "You need a bath, sweetheart. How long you been hittin' the bottle?"

"Long enough to find your son a wife," she snapped, but she tried to pat her hair into place and she took a step backward.

"You don't need to find him no wife," Clay said, tossing his hat on the table. "He'll find one when he's good'n' ready."

"Don't use that cowboy talk on me. You're as slick as oil when you're selling something."

Clay sniffed the air. "Get yourself cleaned up, woman. It's downright embarrassing." With that, Bonnie swore under her breath and left the room. Clay sat down at the table and stretched out his legs.

"Tell me, little lady, are you really the housekeeper in this here asylum?"

Mel smiled at him. "Yes. Would you like a sandwich?"

"What kind?"

"Roast beef."

He seemed to need to think about it, so Mel picked up her knife and continued making sandwiches.

"That's plain, isn't it?"

Mel looked over at him. "I'd say so. Do you have a special diet?"

He winced. "Hell, I guess I do. I'll take one of those sandwiches, no mustard or anything else, and a glass of milk."

"Do you want coleslaw or potato salad with that?"

"No, thank you, ma'am." Clay didn't look pleased about refusing the food. "I think I'd better take it easy."

Mel fixed him a plate, poured a tall glass of milk and served it to him.

"I hate to eat alone," he said, giving her a wink. "You free to sit down and tell me what's going on around here?"

"Do you mean, why is Bonnie wearing Ben's shirt and drinking whiskey?"

"Yep." He took a bite of the sandwich. "For starters. Then you can tell me where my son is."

"I don't know. He left a note," Mel said. Ben's father had the kind of eyes that didn't miss a trick. Mel was willing to bet that not a lot got past Clay. He had the look of a man who knew people.

"It's not like him to leave the ranch in the middle of the summer."

"That's what your wife, ex-wife, said, too."

Clay finished his sandwich in silence, drank his milk and winced. He wiped his face with the napkin Mel furnished and leaned back in his chair. "Not allowed to smoke anymore," he grumbled. "Sure wouldn't mind a good cigar right now."

She didn't think she needed to point out that smoking cigars was bad for his health, so she didn't say anything.

"Tell me about Bonnie," Clay drawled. "She's up to something."

Mel told him about *Texas Men* magazine. Clay swore, apologized and asked if he could have another glass of milk. Mel poured it for him, then settled back in her chair. If he was staying, she'd have to get a room ready, and she didn't know where ex-husbands were supposed to sleep around here.

"Bonnie's answering the letters?"

"Yes."

"There've been women out here?" He looked shocked.

"Two already. Ben wasn't . . . impressed."

"Hell, I could've told her that," Clay roared. "A man likes to pick out his own woman!"

"I would imagine that's true, but Bonnie thinks Ben should be settling down, getting married, starting a family . . ." She stopped, and her hands automatically rested on her belly.

"You're not married, are you?"

"No, but how—"

"No wedding ring," he answered. "And you have the look of a woman on her own," Clay added.

Mel's eyes widened. "What kind of a look is that?"

"Pay no attention to my father, Mel," Ben said, entering the kitchen with long strides. A smile creased his face as he held out his hand to Clay. "The old man's full of shit."

8

BEN TOLD HIMSELF he shouldn't be surprised to see his father sitting in the ranch kitchen. Clay had a habit of showing up at the damnedest times.

He shook his father's hand when what he really wanted to do was take Mel into his arms and tell her he'd missed her. He glanced at her as Clay sat back down at the table.

"Hello, Mel," he said, going to the refrigerator and pouring himself a glass of cold tea.

"Hi, Ben. Do you want something to eat?"

He held up his hand to stop her from getting up. She looked comfortable and he didn't want her to move. "No. I ate on the road." She didn't ask where he'd been. He thought she'd be a little interested. "I was in Dallas," he said.

Clay chuckled. "Sowing some wild oats, son? Good for you!"

Ben winced. He didn't want Mel thinking he'd been sowing anything wild. "Not exactly," he said, sitting down beside Mel. "I had some people to see."

His father didn't believe him, but Ben could tell his old man had decided to change the subject.

"Have you seen your mother?"

"Her car's out front, but I don't know where she is." He turned to Mel. "Did she say why she's here?"

Mel hesitated. "I'm not sure," she said. "Maybe you'd better ask her."

"Jimmy said she's been here for three days."

"Smells like it, too," Clay added. "I hope that woman went to take a shower."

Mel giggled, then looked as if she wished she hadn't. Ben stared at her, then stared some more. She looked pretty good, and he wondered if he smelled cinnamon. "How have you been?" he asked, and she turned to face him.

"Fine."

"Been out to see the pups?"

"I'm better off staying in the kitchen," she said, her gaze steady as she looked at him. "Remember?"

He winced. He didn't want to remember what he'd said. "You're welcome to go anywhere at all on the ranch, Mel. You know that."

She didn't answer, just turned to his father. "Can I get you a piece of pie, Mr. Bradley?"

"Call me Clay. What kind?"

"Peach."

The older man nodded. "That'd be pretty damn hard to refuse."

Mel smiled and got to her feet. She hesitated behind Ben's chair. "What about you, Ben? Want some pie?"

"I can get it myself," he grumbled. He didn't want her waiting on him. He wanted to haul her out to the barn and make love to her. He wanted to find a stall without puppies and he wanted to toss that apron aside and start unbuttoning buttons.

"I'll do it," she insisted, touching his shoulder as if to make him stay in his chair. His skin burned right through the cotton shirt.

Damn, he was glad to be home.

CLAY WAS INVITED to stay for supper. He accepted without pausing, excused himself and, with a wink at his son, sauntered outside for a chat with whoever he met out by the corrals.

Ben pushed his empty plate aside and rested his head on his arm and studied Mel. He'd missed her. He wondered how to tell her. "Anything new happen while I was gone?"

"Your mother holed up in your office and drank your whiskey," she said.

Ben blinked. "Anything else?"

"Not that I know of."

"Jimmy said it was pretty quiet." He searched for something to say. "The new truck broke down, I heard."

"I baked pies for the bake sale in town," she said.

"And the baby? Still kicking?"

"More than ever." She smiled, and Ben's heart flipped over. He wondered what she'd do if he reached out and touched that intriguing mound. He bet his fingers would just about reach around it, like palming a basketball.

"Are you okay?"

"Sure." She stood up then, and reached for the plates. "Why wouldn't I be?" Mel cleared the table and put the dishes in the sink while Ben tried to come up with a reply.

"No reason," he said, following her to the sink. "You're a little thing and you're carrying a baby."

"I'm fine." She had her hands submerged in soapy water and she looked over at him. "Really," she insisted. Then she smiled at him again. "It's nice of you to worry, but—"

He bent to kiss her, and it was like turning on fireworks. Her wet hands went to his shoulders, and his arms wrapped around her body somewhere in the vicinity of her waist. Her lips were just as sweet as he remembered, and the connection between them just as heated and strong.

"Ben?" his mother called. They heard her swift steps on the stairs and broke apart. Mel plunged her hands into the dishwater and Ben backed up a couple of steps as Bonnie entered the kitchen. This time she was dressed for riding. A clean white T-shirt was tucked neatly into her jeans, a red scarf graced her neck, and she held a cowboy hat by its brim.

"Mother?" He found his half-finished glass of tea and picked it up. "What are you doing here?"

Bonnie put her hands on her hips. "Going riding, of course."

"With Clay?"

"Of course not. I need some exercise. And some fresh air, even if it is ninety-eight out there. I've had, um, a busy weekend." She headed toward the door, but stopped before she opened it. "By the way, I'll be staying for dinner, Mel."

"That's fine," Mel said, scrubbing a plate as if her life depended on it.

"Ben?"

He turned to his mother. "What?"

"I'll be expecting to talk to you later, dear."

"Yeah." And he'd be expecting to find lots to do after dinner. In fact, he might be busy until long after sunset. He waited until Bonnie was safely out the door before he turned toward the sink. "Mel?"

She didn't turn around. "What?"

"Can we talk?"

"There's nothing to talk about," she said, not looking at him.

"I missed you," he said.

Mel stopped scrubbing, but she still didn't turn around. "Don't."

"Don't what?" He stepped closer and put his hand on her shoulder when she didn't answer his question. "Look at me," he said, turning her gently to face him. "I missed you while I was gone. Did you miss me?"

"No." She smiled to show she was teasing. "I had your mother to keep me company."

He chuckled and looked at her lips. "Want to go look at puppies tonight?"

The smile faded. "No. That's not a good idea."

"Why not?"

She gave him a serious look, the one that made her look like a schoolteacher. "Take a wild guess."

He asked the question that had bugged him for days. "Are you still in love with him?"

"No."

Which was exactly the answer he wanted to hear. "Then—"

"I'm pretty much through with men," Mel continued. "No offense."

No offense? He wanted her so much that he was in pain from the waist down. He'd thought about no one but her for all the days he'd been in the city trying to have a good time and feeling miserable instead.

"I think I'm better off alone," she added, as if she wasn't carrying someone else inside of her.

"You're not going to be alone for long," he felt obliged to point out.

"No," she said, her eyes serious. "I have to protect both of us, you see."

He didn't see. He only wanted to take her into his arms and make love to her for a long, long while. She didn't kiss like someone who was through with men.

"LIKE OLD TIMES," Jimmy said, passing a bowl of mashed potatoes to Clay.

"Not exactly," Bonnie said, still in her riding clothes.

Clay looked at her and winked. "If this were old times we'd be in the middle of a fight and you'd have throwed me out by now."

"And you'd have deserved it," Bonnie agreed.

Everyone laughed. Supper had turned into a party, though Mel wasn't sure how it came about. Joyce and Jimmy had joined the Bradleys for dinner, and everyone had insisted she set a place for herself at the kitchen table.

Which was okay, considering it wasn't the dining room.

Besides, she wouldn't have missed the ranching stories told by Clay and Jimmy. The two men knew each other well, well enough to finish each other's stories and laugh about earlier times when they were younger.

Even Bonnie seemed less a Dallas society matron than a rancher's wife as she laughed at some of the men's stories. Ben, though obviously he'd heard it all before, egged the men on, and Mel laughed until her sides ached and felt for the first time that she was part of the family.

Which was dangerous. And silly. And not at all sensible. So when Ben offered to help with the dishes, Mel refused. It was time to remember she was the housekeeper. It was time to remember that she was paid for being here.

Ben returned later to ask her to take a walk, and she had to refuse. Only this time he didn't accept her answer. He untied her apron strings and tossed the apron on the freshly wiped counter.

"That's it," he said. "You've worked long enough."

"That's what you pay me for," she reminded him. The sky had grown dark. She had missed the sunset.

"Shut up." He took her elbow and led her onto the screened porch, then waited for her to sit down in the cushioned love seat that rocked, then he sat down beside her. They looked out on the sparkling water in the pool, the pool that Mel had never seen anyone but Lori use.

"Where is everyone?"

"They're over at Jimmy's, playing bridge."

"Bridge?" She couldn't imagine any of them, except perhaps Bonnie, being involved in that particular card game.

"Jimmy would rather play poker, but he's crazy about card games. Clay and Bonnie are sure to get into a brawl if they're each other's partners, but I guess they're going to do it anyway."

"They seem to get along. Have they been divorced long?"

"About twenty years, I guess. They fought like wildcats when they were married, but the past years have mellowed them. They still have the party every year, though."

"The party?"

"To celebrate their divorce," he explained. "It coincides with Labor Day weekend, so they have a barbecue for a couple of hundred people and party till dawn."

She thought that was the strangest thing she'd ever heard.

"Don't worry, though," Ben said, misinterpreting her silence. "Bonnie hires a lot of extra people, plus has it catered. You're not cooking for two hundred people, especially now."

He put his arm along the back of the sofa, and Mel wished she could lean back and rest her head on his shoulder. She resisted.

"You okay?"

"Fine," Mel said, beginning to relax. There was no one to see her sitting on the screened porch in the darkness with her boss. There was no one to see that he was sitting close to her, with his arm stretched behind her. Her day was over, her chores done. Her baby, as if she knew her mother finally had time to pay attention, kicked gently. Mel put her hand on her belly and felt the little nudge under her palm.

"You sure?" He looked down at her hand.

"She's kicking, that's all." She couldn't help it. She leaned back against his shoulder. Ben put his other hand on top of hers.

"Can I?"

She should say no, stop the intimacy right here, but she couldn't. It was tempting to share her baby with someone else. "All right," she said, slipping her hand away and letting Ben splay his fingers over her belly. His hand was warm and the baby, moving again, kicked underneath Ben's fingers.

"Hey!" he said, briefly taking his hand off of her. He replaced it soon enough, when Mel smiled. "She's got quite a kick. You sure it's a girl?"

"No. I just have a feeling." A wish, actually. A boy would need a man around the house. A girl would need a father also, of course, but Mel hoped for a girl. She could teach her to make piecrust and cheer at her soccer games and go shopping for black patent leather shoes.

"Are you really through with men?" His lips were dangerously close to her ear.

"I should be." Mel sighed. "You're not the most reliable species on earth."

"Don't," he said, his voice harsh. He removed his hand and brushed rough fingers against her cheek. "Don't lump me in with him." They both knew who *him* referred to. "I don't deserve it."

They sat in silence for a long moment, and Mel leaned against his shoulder and closed her eyes. She felt his kiss touch her forehead and she knew she should move. She should do a lot of things, she thought, but not one lazy muscle moved to protest when Ben put his hand under her chin and turned her to face him. He kissed her, of course, though Mel tried not to let it affect her.

Which was impossible, since she melted into him the way she always did when he kissed her. It was a most ridiculous reaction, and she didn't remember reacting this way before. She parted her lips at his gentle insistence, and he held her closer against his wide chest. As close as he could with the baby in the way, that is. He kissed her with a startling passion this time, as if he couldn't get enough of her. He kissed her as if he was going to make love to her right there on the porch.

Mel pushed away and looked at the cowboy she'd grown to . . . like. "I won't do this," she whispered.

"It keeps happening," he countered. "Maybe it's supposed to."

"No."

"Yes." He bent to kiss her again, and his lips were hard with passion and wanting. Mel longed to give him what they both wanted, but she couldn't. She wasn't free to make love to him. She was going to have a child. She didn't want to have an affair.

"Ben," she whispered, this time moving away from him. "I'm the housekeeper."

"I know what the hell you are." He frowned at her as she lifted herself from the rocking sofa. "What's that got to do with anything? You think I'm trying to seduce the hired help?"

"That's not—"

"Damn right, it's not," he said, standing in front of her and blocking her path to the kitchen. He was a dark, angry shadow in the dim light, but his voice softened as he added, "I don't know what's happening, either, Mel."

"It has to stop." Mel pushed past him and made her way through the kitchen. She headed to her room and shut the door before she burst into tears. Silly woman, with raging hormones. It was the first time since she'd started working on the Triple Bar S that she'd forgotten to fix the coffee for the morning. Ben Bradley would have to make it himself.

"TROUBLE, SON?"

Ben stood by the fence and looked at the pool. The underwater lights gave it a mysterious glow. "Why in hell do we have this thing?"

His father shrugged. "Your mother thought we needed one when you were small. Trouble was, you always wanted to be on a horse instead." He paused, then tried again. "What's going on around here? Bonnie's up to no good, I can tell. And you look at that little housekeeper like you want to bundle her up and ride off into the sunset."

Ben shrugged. He really didn't want to discuss women with his father, a fast-talking man who'd left a trail of broken hearts all over Texas.

"All right," Clay drawled, pulling a cigar from his pocket and sticking it in his mouth. "Don't talk if you don't want to."

"Aren't you going to light it?"

"Nope. Damn doctors have taken every worthwhile thing away from me, like whiskey and cigars."

"And women?" Ben smiled into the darkness as his father chuckled.

"No damn way, boy. I'll be in my grave before I quit *that* particular activity."

They leaned against the fence for another long moment, neither speaking.

"Your mother's up to something with this magazine thing," Clay said. "And I'll bet a month's profits it ain't got nothin' to do with the housekeeper."

"You're right."

"You better watch yourself, son. Don't do any more kissing on the porch. Why, anyone could be walking around, sneaking a smoke. A person could get the wrong idea, and someone might lose her job."

"No way," Ben said. "Mel's not going anywhere."

"She's pregnant with another man's child."

"I realize that."

"You in love with her?"

"I don't know." He didn't offer the fact that he hadn't had a whole lot of experience with falling in love. Somehow he'd avoided it.

"Bed her and find out," his father drawled.

Ben didn't explain that that was exactly what he was trying to do. "I thought you were playing cards."

"I had the dummy hand, and Bonnie was ticked that I bid her up to four hearts." He shrugged. "It seemed like a good time to get some air." He moved away from the fence. "I'm going to bed. Watch yourself. Bonnie's not giving up on this marriage idea. How in hell did she get you to agree to go along with this bull crap, anyway?"

"She caught me at a weak moment," Ben muttered. He didn't want to discuss King Midas with Clay, knowing how Clay felt about anything that belonged to Ritter. Clay would shoot the prize bull before he'd let him on the Triple Bar S.

"Well, hell, boy," his father said. "I thought I taught you better than that." He shook his head and went into the house, leaving Ben staring at the useless pool. Some of the hands' kids used it during the day. Everyone was welcome. He'd made that clear, but the damn thing remained empty except for water and chlorine.

He didn't want to go into the house. He didn't want to get in that bed alone. He didn't want to spend the night tossing and thinking of Mel.

Ben decided to take one more walk around the barns. He didn't know what was wrong with him, but he sure as hell didn't like it. Lust or love, he was one miserable son of a gun.

"I DON'T THINK this concerns you," Bonnie said, lifting her chin against Clay's hard stare. "Especially since you show up only three times a year. And you still haven't said why you're here three weeks early."

"Felt like it," he replied. "Ben is still my son. I still have some say in what goes on. I still have a room here, remember?" Mel poured him another cup of coffee and watched as he added milk until the liquid reached the top of the mug. She didn't want to be in the kitchen during a family discussion, but she had Bonnie's omelet almost done, and Clay was waiting for French toast.

"You don't know anything about what goes on around here," Bonnie said.

"The hell I don't. What're you up to now, woman?"

"My son's happiness," Bonnie said, raising her voice. "That's all."

Mel wished she was somewhere else. She gripped the spatula and lifted the edges of the omelet away from the pan.

Ben must have made his own coffee this morning. She'd slept until seven-thirty, but after rushing to get dressed and into the kitchen, she found that the others were still asleep. Except Ben, of course. His mug was in the sink, a reminder that she'd missed him. She told herself she was glad.

"You advertise my son like a stud bull and—"

"*Our* son," Bonnie snapped.

"And you invite women here like you was auditioning for some gol-darn play."

"He's lonely."

"Maybe, maybe not." Clay's gaze flickered to Mel as she put Bonnie's breakfast in front of her. "Truth is, it's none of your business."

Bonnie thanked Mel and picked up her fork. "I want him to be happy. That's all."

Mel went to the stove and flipped the French toast. She thought Clay's father had some kind of health problem, considering the bland food he ate. She didn't think anyone else had noticed, but Mr. Bradley didn't eat any salad last night, nor did he drink alcohol or sample any of the salsa Joyce had given them.

Clay leaned back and sipped his coffee. "Then leave him alone."

"No." She looked at Mel and raised her voice. "We'll be having another guest this weekend. I'd like everything to be perfect."

Mel nodded. "Let me know if you want anything special for the meals."

"Thank you. And this omelet is delicious." Bonnie poured more salsa on top of her eggs.

"I'm glad you like it." She finished Clay's French toast and brought it over to him. He didn't look like a man with an appetite. "Mr. Bradley? Can I get you anything else?"

"A little maple syrup, darlin', and a glass of milk. And you're supposed to call me Clay."

He winked at her, making Mel smile. Ben's father was a real charmer, but she couldn't picture him married to Bonnie. They were too much alike, stubborn and independent, with a wild streak a foot wide and a mile long.

She didn't think Ben inherited that wildness, but she didn't know what he'd been doing in Dallas, either. She didn't really think he'd been looking for trouble, though. If he wanted trouble, he could have stayed on the ranch and let Bonnie find it for him.

MEL INTENDED to avoid Ben. She really did, she told herself. But the damn cowboy made it hard to ignore him. At first he'd stayed away, which was fine with Mel. Easier on the hormones, of course. Easier on her heart rate.

That lasted one day.

Then Ben was back, sitting in her kitchen, drinking her coffee, eating her cinnamon rolls. And not saying much, that was for sure. On the second day it started to make her crazy. She was too aware of him. Even being in the same room set her nerves jingling and made her think of stolen kisses and being held in those strong arms.

Clay had taken over the spare room downstairs next to Ben's office, and Bonnie went to Dallas. She'd promised to return on Friday. This time, she'd informed everyone, she was going to make sure everything went perfectly. Clay had laughed, and Ben just shook his head.

Neither man seemed concerned, but Mel wondered what kind of woman Bonnie would choose next. She wouldn't be plain and she wouldn't be pregnant, that was for sure.

Thursday came, and Mel escaped to town. It was her half day off, so she took advantage of the free time by depositing her paycheck, visiting the library and browsing through the toy section of the local hardware store. She resisted buying a Tonka dump truck and a Fisher Price doll. She stopped by the Hair Hut and asked if anyone had time to trim her hair, and a hefty redhead named Gert picked up a pair of scissors and told her to sit down in the middle chair.

Then she bought a new lipstick at the drugstore, picked up the special groceries needed for the weekend and headed to the ranch. The men were nowhere around, which was fine with Mel. It didn't take long to unload the groceries, especially when she left the heavy stuff—like detergent and bottles of soda pop—for Ben to bring in later. She fixed herself a glass of iced tea, took her library books and went into her room. Stretched out on the bed, shoes kicked off and the shades drawn, Mel promptly closed her eyes and began to dream of babies riding horses.

"THINK I SHOULD check on her?"

"It's her day off, isn't it?"

"Yeah."

"Then let her enjoy it. Women like their time to do women things." Clay put his dirty plate in the dishwasher and looked at his watch. "I told Jimmy I'd be over at nine to go over the plans for the new barn. He wants another opinion."

"Go ahead."

"You don't want to come, too?"

"No. I'll take the night off," Ben said, staying seated at the kitchen table. What the hell were women things?

Clay hesitated by the door. "We'll most likely head into town later to play a little pool. You want us to come by and get you?"

"No." He didn't want to play pool or look at building plans. He wanted to see Mel and make sure she was all right. He'd hauled the groceries from the station wagon and heated up the lasagna she'd left in the refrigerator and now he wanted to see her. He'd been avoiding her. She'd been avoiding him.

If he was in love with her he wanted to find out. So he walked down the hall to her room. No light shone from underneath the closed door. No sound came from within. Mel could be sick or hurt or...asleep. He knocked softly, but got no answer. She must have been tired after going to town. He would have to make sure he went with her from now on. She was too far along in her pregnancy to be carrying groceries.

Ben paced in the hall for a few minutes. What if she needed him? What if she'd called his name while he was eating dinner and he hadn't heard? He stopped in front of her door again and pressed his ear against the wood. Nothing. No sound at all.

She could be unconscious. She could be in labor. She could need him. Beads of sweat broke out on his forehead. He hesitated for a second, then turned the doorknob and pushed the door open a few inches. He peered inside, hoping it wasn't a mistake. He wasn't in the habit of going into a woman's room without an invitation. In fact, he thought, he hadn't been invited anywhere in one hell of a long time.

Ben eased the door open wide enough to slip into the dark room and stopped, letting his eyes adjust to the dark. He could make out Mel's body on the bed and, as he tiptoed closer, he heard the faint sound of rhythmic breathing. She lay on her side facing the door, and her eyes were closed. She was asleep. He had worried for nothing. He expelled his breath in relief, and she opened her eyes and blinked when she saw him.

"Ben?"

"Yeah." He stood frozen by the bed, when he wanted to touch her face and brush a tendril of hair from her cheek. "Sorry," he managed to say. "I thought I'd better check on you."

Mel yawned sleepily. She wasn't wearing her glasses, which made her look different. "Is it late?"

"Almost nine."

She yawned again. "Sorry." She smiled. "I guess I was more tired than I thought."

"I'll let you go back to sleep," he offered. He took one step closer.

"Okay."

He sat on the bed instead. There was just enough room. Mel turned on her back and looked at him.

"I'm seven months pregnant," she announced, like it was a late-breaking news report.

"I can count." He leaned down and daringly planted a kiss on her belly. "Does that mean we can't make love?"

"It means I don't look like Tessie Mae."

She wore one of those pink dresses, and he thought she looked just fine. "I'm glad," he said, and he meant it. He wrapped his fingers around one slender ankle and moved his hand higher, to her calf. Her skin was warm and smooth, and he dared to touch higher, above her knee to a slender thigh.

"Ben," she said, and he stopped his explorations. But he didn't take his hand from her thigh.

"What?"

"I don't know what we're doing," she whispered.

"I do," he said. "We're doing what we've both been thinking about since the first time I kissed you."

She swallowed hard, and her gaze held his. "I look like a beached whale."

"I think you're beautiful."

"I'm not," she said, and tears welled in her eyes. "Especially not now."

"You are beautiful," Ben insisted. "Don't cry." He bent and kissed her gently. Then he looked at her again and smiled. "I can prove it."

"How?" She smiled.

He traced the line of her jaw with one finger, then touched her lips. "It's going to take a while," he drawled. "Maybe all night."

Her arms went around his neck, and Ben tucked one arm under her knees and the other around her back. He lifted her from the bed, and she held on to him. "Where—"

"Not here," he said, moving toward the door. She was light and delicate in his arms. "Upstairs. My room."

It was easy to carry her through the hall and up the stairs to the wide bedroom that faced the front of the house and overlooked the road and pastures beyond. He set her gently on his king-size bed, then leaned over to turn on the bedside lamp.

"No." Mel touched his arm. "Please."

"All right." He sat beside her on the bed and started unbuttoning his shirt, but she surprised him by pushing his fingers aside and unfastening the shirt herself.

She smiled at him. "I've thought about doing that," Mel confessed, and he ached from wanting her. He pulled off his boots and tossed them aside, along with his socks.

He managed to undress and toss the rest of his clothes on the floor in a record-breaking amount of time before turning to Mel.

"Your turn," he said, reaching for her buttons with a hand he wished wouldn't tremble. God, he didn't want to hurt her. She helped him, and her fingers shook, too, until he clasped her hand and brought her fingers to his lips to kiss.

He didn't know how they managed to pull the covers down and slide between the sheets. He only knew he couldn't wait to stretch out beside her naked body and feel her skin. She lay on her side facing him, the uncertain expression back in her eyes. "What's wrong?" he asked.

"This is frightening."

Ben inched closer so that her belly touched his and he reached out and lifted one perfect breast in the palm of his hand. "How so?"

"It feels too...good," she whispered, and his lips found hers in the darkness. He kissed her for long moments, kissed her to give her time to get used to lying beside him. To give himself time to believe that this was really happening.

He touched her, between her thighs and higher. She gasped when his fingers parted her and found the wetness there.

"Am I going too fast?" he whispered.

She shook her head. "Not fast enough."

"I don't have to . . . enter you to make love, Mel. Just kissing you, and holding you—"

"It's all right. The doctor said it was."

"I don't want to hurt you."

She caressed his chest, smoothing her palms over his skin. "You won't hurt me, Ben."

Ben moved above her, positioning himself carefully so he wouldn't hurt the baby before entering her. He paused to look down at her as he slowly pushed inside her. She was wet and warm, sweetly tight around him. Her hands touched his hips, guiding him closer. He braced himself with his arms and kept his weight from her as he moved cautiously into her. She felt so damn good, with all that womanly warmth surrounding him, pulling him deeper within her. He made love to her until heard her little cry, felt her climax around him as he came deep inside of her.

When he could breath again, he reluctantly withdrew from that sweet warmth and lay on his side. He tucked her into his body and fit her to him, so that her buttocks were tucked against his partial arousal. His hand was free to pull the sheet over their shoulders, and he kissed her neck.

She was asleep in minutes, but Ben lay awake and held her.

He didn't know when he would ever be given such a gift again.

9

MEL WOKE to find herself tucked snugly in Ben's arms. It was a wonderful feeling, pressed against a man's body, being held in the middle of the night. She would have turned to face him, but he stopped her. She was ready for him again, so he fit himself inside her and made love to her without worrying about hurting the baby. She didn't know why she felt so sexy or so content. Hormones, she reminded herself after the particularly wonderful conclusion to their lovemaking, were powerful things. It couldn't be anything else, of course. She was too smart to fall in love again.

Mel turned carefully and saw that Ben was asleep. He needed a shave, and his hair was rumpled and, even if she did like looking at him, she was older and wiser and going to be a mother in ten weeks. She definitely knew better than to think she was in love.

Of course she did.

"MORNIN', DARLIN'," Ben said, striding into the kitchen. He looked like the cat who ate the canary this morning, and Mel's heart flipped over just at the sight of him.

"Shh," she whispered, knowing Clay was asleep down the hall. At least, she hoped he was asleep. The older man was an early riser, a habit from his cowboy days, he'd explained once. She hoped he hadn't heard her stumble back to her room this morning. She couldn't see much without her glasses, and she'd stubbed her toe twice. Then she'd hurried to take a shower and fix her hair. She didn't want to look like she'd had sex, but when she'd studied herself in the mirror she was actually glowing.

Hormones again, she reminded herself. Some pregnant women were radiant.

"No," Ben said, coming up behind her and wrapping his arms around her as she tried to scramble eggs. He kissed her neck, and Mel blushed and moved away.

"Don't, Ben. Your father—"

He turned her to face him. "Is asleep. I heard him snoring."

"He's usually awake by now."

"Maybe he had a late night." He planted a light kiss on her lips. "Like we did. Why did you leave me?"

"I thought it was best."

"Not for me," he said, lowering his voice. "I wanted to wake up with you in my arms."

"You did. Once," she reminded him, returning to the eggs. How did he expect her to cook breakfast if he continued to kiss her?

"Not enough." He sighed, moving away and pouring himself a cup of coffee. "I'm going to be worthless today."

He wasn't the only one. She'd be lucky if she didn't fall asleep by noon, and there were a million things to do. She needed to make a list. She poured the eggs in the skillet and reached for her own cup of coffee.

"Go back to bed," Ben said, taking the spatula out of her hand. "I can make my own breakfast."

"I'll take a nap later," she promised, taking the spatula back. "Your eggs are going to burn, and I forgot about the bacon."

"Then I'll have toast," he said, watching her scrape the eggs onto his plate. "Are you going to eat?"

"I did already."

"Then sit with me."

She found a pad of paper and a pen by the phone. "I have too much to do."

"Sit down and make your list. What's got you into a tizzy?"

Mel sat across from him and wondered what it would be like to spend every night in his arms. What would it be like to make love to him when she had a flat stomach? He was a generous lover, and she wanted to be generous back, but she wouldn't give herself that chance. It happened once. Well, twice. And it wasn't going to happen again.

"Mel?"

He interrupted her promise to herself. Mel looked at the blank piece of paper, then at Ben. "What?"

"I asked what's going on."

"It's Friday. You're getting company, remember?"

Ben leaned back in his chair. "Oh, hell. Another woman?"

Mel couldn't help smiling at the disgusted look on his face. "Some men would think they had a pretty good thing going, with different women coming to visit for the weekend."

He glared at her, but she knew he wasn't really angry. "*Some* men would be happy with what they've got."

Mel went back to her list. Tessie Mae and Candy had proved to be demanding houseguests, leaving Ben disgusted with his mother's good intentions. What would the next one be like?

THERE WAS NO ONE to answer the door. Mel, hot and rumpled from baking a cake and boiling macaroni for a chilled salad, lumbered to the front door. She swung it open and saw a tall, gorgeous blond woman standing on the sidewalk.

"Hi," the woman said, showing a set of perfect white teeth. "I'm Carla Cassidy. I think I'm expected."

"Come on in." Mel stepped outside to help with the luggage, but Carla shooed her away.

"Don't you dare, not in your condition," she said, picking up two matching bags and stepping into the foyer. "When are you due?"

"Mid-October. I'm Mel, by the way. I'm the housekeeper here." *And I sleep with the boss.* She didn't want to envy the woman's flat stomach, or the way she could tuck her white cotton shirt into well-worn jeans. Or the casual way she wore expensive boots. Carla was probably thirty, older than the others. She even had tiny laugh lines around her blue eyes, and she wore just enough makeup to look like she cared.

Mel looked over her shoulder to see if Carla had brought her own horse. An immaculate silver Mercedes sat in the driveway. Mel turned away and closed the door. "Come on in," she said, gesturing toward the living room. "What would you like to drink?"

"Not a thing," she said. "Just tell me where my room is and I'll get these bags out of your way."

"Upstairs," Mel answered, her heart sinking to her rather tight shoes. It was nice of this visitor to keep her from climbing a set of steps. "Second door on the left. It's the room with the yellow-and-white wallpaper."

"Great. Thanks." Carla gave her another smile and headed up the stairs. Mel went into the kitchen and sat down. Maybe leaving was the answer. How could she watch Ben with another woman, a *perfect* woman, and not burst into tears?

Her doctor had assured her it was natural to be more emotional, but was it natural to feel an overwhelming envy of anyone who could zip up her jeans?

Mel tried to rest her forehead on the table, but she couldn't bend over that far. Talk about depressing, she thought, pushing her chair back and contemplating the size of her abdomen. Maybe this afternoon Carla would swear, or flirt, or shoot something Ben didn't want shot. There was always hope.

"Hey, darlin'," Clay called, sliding the door open and stepping inside. He was covered in dust and grinning from ear to ear. As usual, good-natured charm oozed from every pore. "What's the matter? You look sadder than a calf at brandin' time."

Mortified to be caught moping, Mel pasted a smile on her face. "I'm fine. Just feeling a little like a walking sack of potatoes."

"You're still a little thing," he said, giving her a wink. "You should have seen Bonnie before she had Ben. Swelled up like a balloon, from her ankles to her neck."

Mel laughed. "I can't picture that."

"And she turned mean, too." He tilted his hat from his forehead and winced.

"What's the matter?"

He rubbed his stomach. "Nothing I can't handle, hon. I'm going to have a glass of something cold—no, don't get up—and then head out to help Lori with that damn chestnut horse. You have any of those cinnamon rolls?" He went over to the refrigerator and poured himself a tall glass of milk.

"I, um, didn't have time to bake this morning. Did you know we have company?"

"Yeah. I saw Bonnie's car heading up the road. She must've been going seventy."

"No, I mean—"

A light voice called from the hall. "Mel? Hello?"

"In here," Mel answered, getting to her feet, but Carla appeared in the kitchen doorway.

"I thought I heard voices," she said. She stuck out one hand and smiled at Clay. "You must be Ben. I'm Carla Cassidy. Thanks for inviting me out to your ranch."

Clay's smile was genuine, Mel noted, and he took her hand into his big brown one. "My pleasure," he drawled, sounding like a Texas cattle baron.

"He's not—" she began, but the front door slammed and Bonnie's heels clicked across the tiled floor.

The older man didn't release Carla's hand. "I'm not Ben, I'm the boy's father," he told her, making Ben sound about twelve years old.

"Am I late? I'm so sorry." Bonnie hurried in, her gauzy white skirt swirling around her ankles. She wore a white shirt similar to Carla's, and a large silver-and-turquoise necklace added a festive touch. But Clay didn't turn to look at her, though he did release Carla's hand as she turned toward the older woman.

"Mrs. Bradley?"

Bonnie looked as if she had discovered gold. "Call me Bonnie. You're Carla. Welcome to the Triple Bar S."

"Thank you. I just met your husband and—"

"We're divorced," Clay drawled.

"Very divorced," Bonnie agreed. She took Carla by the elbow. "Have you met my son yet?"

"No. I just got settled, actually. You have a beautiful home."

"Why, thank you. I'll let Ben give you a tour of the ranch as soon as we find him." She turned to Mel. "Have you seen him, Mel?"

"Not since breakfast." She'd been avoiding him, knowing she would sink into his arms at any available opportunity, knowing she could make a fool of herself without half trying.

"Come on, Carla," Clay said. "I'll take you outside. We'll hunt him down and let him know you're here."

Bonnie hesitated, then agreed. "Go ahead. I'll change and catch up with you. You said in your letter that you like to ride?"

"I grew up on a ranch outside of Austin."

"Yes, of course." Ben's mother looked as if she was going to burst with excitement. "Go on," she said, waving her hand. "I'll find you later. We'll pick out a horse for you to use while you're here."

Clay opened the door. "I'll bet you like 'em with a little pep."

Carla smiled one of her perfect smiles. "How'd you guess?"

They disappeared outside, and Bonnie and Mel watched as the couple took the path to the barns. Ranger greeted Carla like a long-lost friend, and Carla petted her as if she'd owned the dog for years. "I hope Ben is out there." She turned to Mel. "What do you think? Better than the others?"

"A hundred times better." Mel sighed and started to feel sorry for herself again. "Ben is going to like her."

"YOU LIKE HER, don't you?" Bonnie whispered.

"Sure." Ben pulled on a clean shirt. He would have to start locking his bedroom door. "She hasn't cussed, grabbed my crotch or pulled out a gun. Why wouldn't I like her?"

"Oh, stop exaggerating," his mother said, stepping into his room. "We had a lovely ride, and she seemed to like the ranch."

Ben worked on his buttons. This had gone far enough. He was going to put a stop to this now, before it went any further. Before innocent people got hurt. He wanted Mel. Only Mel. He didn't know what that meant yet, but he'd sure like some time to figure it out.

He'd like some time to convince the little lady herself, and he didn't think it was going to be easy. He'd caught her at a weak moment last night, and he'd carried her to his bed and he'd made love to her twice, and today she wouldn't let him near her without putting up a fuss. "I don't understand women," he said, then realized he'd spoken out loud.

"Of course you don't," his mother agreed. "That's why you have me."

"This has gone far enough. All bets are off. Send her away. Tell her I have to go to Dallas or New York or France."

"No way," Bonnie said. "You can't squirm out of this now that I'm about to win. We shook hands."

"I can do any damn thing I please."

"Three women," she said, looking as if she wanted to take him over her knee like she'd done a few times when he was little. "You said you'd behave. And I said if you did I'd get King Midas for you. Have you forgotten?"

Yeah, he'd forgotten, all right. Bull sperm hadn't entered his mind for weeks and was most likely the last thing he cared to consider in all of this. He supposed he owed her something. After all, she'd hired Mel, hadn't she? "All right. I'll be a gentleman," he said. "For the weekend." He could live through a weekend, but on Monday he was going to talk to Mel and they were going to have one hell of a long conversation. He thought about taking her to bed again, and his spirits lifted.

Bonnie patted his arm. "You're so handsome when you smile. You should do it more often."

MEL WOULDN'T join them for dinner, which annoyed Ben so much he wanted to haul her out to the barn so he could yell without anyone listening. But he didn't. He didn't want to embarrass her and he didn't want anyone to know they'd made love. It was no one's business anyway. And he didn't want people talking until he'd figured out what was going on.

Mel wasn't helping him figure it out.

He wanted her in his bed. Every night. But he didn't know how to get her there. He didn't have much experience with women. And he had no experience at all with pregnant ones. So he was polite to Carla, who seemed nice enough. Clay filled in the conversation and Bonnie, who never needed any help talking, did her share to entertain. As soon as he could escape, Ben hurried into the kitchen. Mel had made a pot of coffee. A lemon cake had been cut into thick wedges, dessert plates stacked neatly on the kitchen table. He looked further and spotted Mel on the porch. He stepped closer, intending to open the door and join her, but he stopped before pushing the screen door open. She was curled up on the love seat, and her eyes were closed. Sound asleep, he'd bet, and he knew the reason.

He served dessert himself, ignoring his mother's beaming expression and Clay's amused grin. Then he got Clay to tell that old rodeo story, which led to the one about Cody, Wyoming, and Clay's outriding the future governor of Montana. That killed about half an hour, until Bonnie grew edgy and suggested a walk. Ben agreed, guiding his guest and his parents out the door before anyone could question why they were leaving through the front entrance. He would do his best to let Mel sleep. God knows, it was all his fault that she hadn't had enough rest last night.

Ben left the others discussing horses while he hurried back to the house. Mel was still curled up on the sofa, so he scooped her into his arms and carried her to her room.

"Ben?" Her voice was sleepy, and she didn't open her eyes.

"Yeah." He shoved the covers aside and laid her on the bed as gently as he could.

"What are you doing?" She opened her eyes and yawned.

"You fell asleep on the porch."

She struggled to sit up. "I've got to clean—"

He stopped her. "I'll take care of it."

"Bonnie—"

"Will be told you weren't feeling well and she'll understand." He removed her sandals, covered her with the flowered sheet and kissed her on the forehead. "Close your eyes, darlin', and go back to sleep. I'll shut the door on the way out."

MEL MADE CINNAMON ROLLS Sunday morning. It was a celebration of sorts, she figured. Perfect Carla would be leaving and, although the woman hadn't done anything but be pleasant, Mel still couldn't help twinges of jealousy whenever Carla talked to Ben.

Though she told herself that Ben should find someone he could love. Someone he could marry. Someone whose pants had a zipper instead of an elastic waistband. Someone whose baby would also belong to Ben.

The three Bradleys ate breakfast in the kitchen, but since Ben was the last one to arrive, Mel hadn't had a chance to thank him for helping her last night. The kitchen had been clean this morning, and she knew who was responsible.

Ben poured himself another cup of coffee and walked to the table. "What time is Carla leaving? I want to make sure I say goodbye."

"Didn't I tell you?" Bonnie began, taking a sip of her coffee before continuing. Her son and ex-husband waited with identical impatient expressions.

"Tell us what?" Ben asked, frowning as if he knew he wouldn't like the answer.

"I invited Carla to stay for a week," she announced. "I realized, with the other guests, that two days wasn't nearly long enough to make a connection."

Mel's heart sank. She opened the dishwasher and began tossing dishes inside, whether they were dirty or not. It was something to do.

"There's no so-called connection now," Ben was saying. "I've told you that."

"How could there be, in only a weekend?"

Clay cleared his throat. "On the other hand, Bon, you and I knew within five minutes."

"And look where it got us," she scoffed, her gaze returning to her son. "These things take time."

Her ex-husband shrugged. "Anyone can make a mistake."

Mel grabbed a damp sponge and started scrubbing the counters. A week. A lot could happen in a week. Look what had happened in one night, she reminded herself. She'd let Ben carry her up to his bed, and the world had changed. Now it shifted into position again, and she was going to fade into the background and cook dinner and do dishes and bake bread and get out of here as soon as possible.

"Give up, Mother," Ben said. He didn't look happy, Mel noted. In fact, he looked as if he would like to strangle something. Or someone.

"More coffee, anybody?" she asked, picking up the carafe.

"Now, Benjamin," Bonnie began. Mel filled her cup and tried to catch Ben's eye, but he was focused on his mother.

"That wasn't part of the deal," he said. "I'm not entertaining one of your guests for a week. I have work—"

"Good morning," Carla said, stepping into the room.

"Good morning," Bonnie said, turning to her guest.

"I'm sorry I'm late." She walked over to the table and sat in the empty chair beside Clay.

"No such thing as sleeping too late on Sunday," he told her. "Didn't you know that?"

She smiled at him and thanked Mel for the cup of coffee placed near her elbow. "Would anyone mind if I went riding today?"

Bonnie looked at her son. "Ben? I'm afraid I have plans for this afternoon, but you don't have anything to do today, do you?"

"As a matter of fact," Ben began, but his father interrupted him.

"Let's ride out to the old homestead," he suggested. "I'm sure Carla would appreciate a little family history."

"I think that sounds wonderful." Carla smiled at everyone. "If it's not too much trouble."

Clay smiled at their guest. "No trouble at all, hon. We'll make ourselves a lunch and have us a nice long ride."

"Maybe the young people would like to be by themselves," Bonnie said, giving her ex-husband a warning look.

Mel dropped a handful of silverware on the floor. Ben stepped over to help her pick it up.

"I don't want to interfere with Ben's work," Carla said. "That's really not necessary at all."

Ben stood up, tossed the silverware in the sink and nodded toward his guest. "A picnic sounds fine."

It was Clay's turn to frown.

BONNIE, promising to return for supper Friday night with a guest list and a menu, left for Dallas. Carla ate a roll, then went outside to select a horse to ride. Which left one too many people in the kitchen, Ben figured, watching Mel slice fruit into a plastic bowl.

"Son, I've got a solution to our troubles," Clay drawled.

"Our troubles?" Ben echoed.

Clay glanced at Mel and then lowered his voice. "Truth is, you and I both know that you're no more interested in a picnic with Carla than you are in hog-tying a dinosaur."

"And?"

He winked at his son. "I'll make your excuses to the lady."

"Think she'll mind?"

Clay smiled, a man confident of his ability to charm. "I'll make sure she doesn't."

"I'll bet you will," Ben said, finally catching on. Come to think of it, the old man wasn't really that old. Fifty-five, actually. "You know, you never said why you came home."

"An ulcer," Clay confessed. "Just keep it under your hat. The doc told me to get some rest and eat properly and I'd be fine."

"You sure?"

"Hell, son." Clay winked and stood up, a tall man with wide shoulders and a twinkle in his eyes. "Do I look like a man in pain?"

"No, I guess you don't."

Clay put his hat on his head and called goodbye to Mel. "I'll be back in a few minutes for that lunch, hon."

"It's almost ready," she said, opening the refrigerator.

Clay turned to his son. "A little advice," he said, lowering his voice. "There are only a couple of things you have to be scared of in this here life—a decent woman and being left afoot."

Ben chuckled. "Then I should be terrified," he admitted.

"You'll live," his father said, and went out the door.

Ben turned to watch Mel construct sandwiches and wrap them in plastic. She was trying real hard to ignore him, but he knew she knew he was there. And she knew he wasn't going away, either.

"When are you leaving?" she finally asked. "I'll have this ready in a few minutes."

"I'm not going."

Mel looked up, clearly surprised. "But I thought—"

"You thought I'd rather spend the afternoon with Carla than you?" He came over to her and removed the knife from her hand. There was no sense taking chances.

"Clay volunteered to take her off my hands for the entire afternoon."

"That was nice of him."

"Yeah." He bent down to kiss her, but Mel backed up.

"No," she said. "We can't do that."

"Why not?"

"Because I'm the housekeeper," she said quite firmly.

"So?"

"The *pregnant* housekeeper," she said, and her eyes filled with tears.

"Aw, honey, why don't you tell me who he is so I can go after him for you?"

She sniffed. "He didn't want the baby. Or me. We even . . . signed papers, so he would never be responsible." Her chin quivered. "We were together a long time, and he left, just like that."

"Then I don't want you near him," Ben said, wrapping her in his arms. "Don't cry."

"I'm not crying," she said, her voice quavering.

"You don't need the bastard." *Not when you have me.* He didn't say it aloud, but he wondered if he meant it. He wondered if this was real, if this was love, after all. He wanted to take anything or anyone who hurt Mel and break them into tiny pieces.

"I know."

"Not now, not ever," he added. He wanted to hand her his heart and tell her he'd never given it away before. He wanted to carry her off to bed and show her how he felt.

"Come on," he said, setting her away from him. "I'll help you pack up the lunch. The sooner they're gone, the sooner you can rest up."

She reached for the bread. "I don't need to rest up."

"Well, I do." He grinned. "I tossed and turned last night like I was on the ground. All of a sudden I don't like sleeping alone."

Mel took off her glasses and wiped the fringe of tears from the bottom of the frames. "I don't know what's the matter with me," she confessed. "I never cry."

She needed him, Ben figured, picking up the knife and dipping it into the mustard jar. She needed a man in her life, and he was just the person to take care of Mel. Whether she knew it or not. "I have an idea," he said, keeping his voice casual. "Let's go to the movies."

"Where?"

"There's a matinee on weekends in Rose River. We can get popcorn and, if you're real lucky, we can sit in the back row and hold hands."

She laughed. "Hold hands in the movies? I haven't done that in years."

"We can kiss, too," he offered, the idea appealing to him more and more. "It will be dark and cool, and no one will know us."

"What's playing?"

"Does it matter?"

"I guess not. As long as it's not too violent," Mel said. She tossed a couple of apples into a sack. "And nothing too sad."

"No blood, no tears," he repeated, looking for the Sunday newspaper in the pile of papers on the counter. "We should be able to find something. I think Clint Eastwood has a new Western out."

"I'll close my eyes during the gunfights," Mel promised. She looked happy, Ben noted, so his idea must have been a good one. He wanted to get her off the ranch, away from being a housekeeper, away from Carla and Bonnie and Clay and everyone else on the ranch. He wanted her all to himself today.

He wanted her all to himself tonight, too, but a man had to take one step at a time. He wasn't going to give up. There was no room around the campfire for a quitter's bedroll.

10

Mel took a seat on the aisle in the back row while Ben went to buy popcorn and drinks. She preferred the aisle, in case she had to get up in the middle of the movie and go to the bathroom. She liked the back row for the same reason.

"Mel?"

She knew that voice. Mel turned to see Bonnie standing in the aisle. "Bonnie?"

"I, uh, decided not to go to Dallas yet."

"I thought I'd take the afternoon off," Mel said at the same time.

"Good," Bonnie said, but she looked flustered. A stocky man stood behind her, his hand resting possessively on the small of her back. He had a big square face, weathered skin and the physique of a man who worked hard. Another cattle baron, Mel decided. His Western shirt was neatly pressed and tucked into dark pants. Mel tried not to stare at the gleaming gold belt buckle, but it looked like the etched head of a Texas longhorn.

"We'd better find a seat, darlin'," the man said, giving Mel a smile. "She likes to sit in the front so no one sits in front of her."

"I hope you enjoy the movie," Mel said. *I hope Ben doesn't come back yet.* How would she explain she had a date with the boss? How would Ben explain he wasn't taking Carla on a picnic? She didn't think they had seen Ben, or they would have said something. Mel watched the older couple go down the aisle to the front row of the theater and settle themselves in their seats as the lights dimmed and the first preview of coming attractions began.

"Hey, lady," Ben drawled. "I've brought food."

Mel stood up and moved into the aisle, looking to see if Bonnie had turned around. She hadn't. In fact, she'd sunk low in her seat as if to disappear. Ben sat beside Mel and angled his long legs to the side while Mel sat down again.

"What are you looking at?"

"Your mother is here."

Ben swore softly, and Mel hoped no one heard. The theater was surprisingly crowded, especially with teenagers, who looked like they had nothing else to do. She suspected everyone else was looking for a cool place to spend a couple of hours.

"Where?"

"In front. I think she has a date."

"Probably," he said. "She's got men trailing her everywhere."

Mel didn't point out that this particular man didn't look as if he trailed after anything but cattle, but she kept her mouth closed. "We can't let her see us together."

"She'll have to get used to it sometime." He handed her a soda and a fistful of napkins, then placed a gallon of popcorn on his knee so she could reach it easily.

"There's nothing to get used to," Mel pointed out.

"She has to know sooner or later."

"Not necessarily," Mel whispered, helping herself to popcorn. "Besides, you're supposed to be on a picnic with Carla."

"Hell. I forgot."

"It was nice of your father to take her instead."

"Yeah. Real nice." She wondered why he chuckled.

"I think we should leave," Mel said, watching the silhouette of Bonnie's head at the front of the theater. "Don't you?"

Just at that moment the movie started. "Have some popcorn and relax, sweetheart. We'll get out of here as soon as the movie's over."

"But—"

"Shh," he said, giving her a wink. "You're missing the beginning of the movie."

Mel looked at the screen and watched Clint Eastwood step down from a horse that looked like it had traveled across most of Texas without stopping. She took another handful of popcorn and tried to relax. She wasn't doing anything wrong, after all. Just sitting in a dark movie theater with a man she was falling in love with.

She was insane. Stupid and insane.

Looking mean, Clint Eastwood pulled out his gun, and Mel closed her eyes.

HE BOUGHT HER ICE CREAM after the movie. She hadn't wanted to go into the Pastime, of course. He'd told her three or four times that Bonnie wouldn't step foot in the café.

"My mother would prefer a gin and tonic instead," he said. "She's probably at Sloppy Joe's or the Watering Hole." Then he'd watched Mel relax a little more.

"You don't think she saw us?"

"Nope."

The waitress set big hot fudge sundaes and long-handled spoons in front of them, then hurried off to the next customer. Mel picked up her spoon and dipped it into the whipped cream. She looked happy. He liked making her happy, he realized. And she was happy about the simplest things.

Like clean kitchens and ice cream and slow horses.

But she wasn't happy about him. He was smart enough to realize that, but he wasn't smart enough to understand why. They ate their sundaes in companionable silence. Or at least he thought it was like that. Maybe she was mad at him and he wasn't catching on.

Mel smiled then, and took a sip of water. "I think that was better than the popcorn."

"I would've bought you dinner instead." *I would've bought you the moon if it was for sale.*

She shook her head. "We should get back. Tomorrow's my day off, not today. And Carla and Clay will want dinner."

"They can go out to eat," he muttered. "Let's stay in town and go out to dinner."

Mel smiled again. "I'm full. Let's go home?"

"Home," he repeated, liking the way she'd said it. "Sure." He stood up, picked up the check, then set a ten-dollar bill on the table to cover the charges and a big tip. He'd liked the way the waitress had left them alone. "We're out of here," he said, taking her hand and helping her to her feet.

"Ben!" a man hollered, waving from across the room.

Ben had no choice but to nod and try to look a little bit friendly. Pete Johnson had a mouth on him. The man just didn't know when to shut up. Pete, easily three hundred pounds and an ex-lineman for Texas A&M, thundered across the restaurant toward them.

"Hey," he said, grinning. "I haven't seen you in a hell—'scuse me, ma'am—of a long time." His gaze dropped to Mel's rounded stomach. "Or longer," he added, looking at Ben.

"Hey, Pete." The men shook hands, then Ben made the introductions.

"Mel, this is Pete Johnson, an old friend of mine."

Mel shook hands with him. "Mel," he repeated. "It's a pleasure." Then he turned to Ben. "I didn't know you got married."

Ben ignored the comment. "How's everything out on your place? The kids all right?"

"Yeah. Jane's sure looking forward to the barbecue. We got the invitation a couple of days ago, and she's been talking about it ever since."

"Good." He put his hand on the small of Mel's back and nudged her forward. If they started moving toward the door, maybe Pete would get the hint that they were on their way somewhere important.

He didn't. "We've got to get together, Ben, have a drink. You'll have to tell me when you got—"

"Yeah," he said, cutting Pete off before he could ask any more questions and embarrass Mel. "Come to the shindig early, before all of the best whiskey is gone," he offered, guiding Mel around the man. "We're out of here, Pete. Gotta get the little lady home."

Pete winked. "I know how that is," he roared, clapping Ben on the back. Ben stepped aside and headed toward the door.

"Why did you do that?" Mel said, once they were walking down the sidewalk.

"Do what?"

"Let him think we were married?"

Ben shrugged. "I let him think what he wanted to think. Besides, it wasn't his business."

"You should have told him I was the housekeeper," she said, sounding angry. "You should have told him the truth."

The truth, Ben thought. Now that sounded serious. He adjusted his long stride to Mel's short steps as they walked to the truck. She didn't wait for him to open the door and climbed in as best she could without help. Ben

watched her and wondered if she was going to stay mad
for a long time. He shut her door for her, then got in on
his own side. He turned the engine on, turned the air-
conditioning to high, rolled down his window and tilted
his hat back.

"It wasn't any of Pete's business," Ben repeated.
Maybe she hadn't heard him the first time.

"This is all wrong," Mel said, her voice very small, so
he turned to her and touched her chin so she would have
to look at him.

"No," he said.

"Yes," she argued. "I'm going to have a baby. I'm going to be somebody's mother. I can't do this."

"Do what?"

She was silent then, but she had that familiar determined look on her face. "I think we'd better get back to
the ranch."

"In a minute," Ben said, leaning forward in front of the
cool air blowing from the vents. He touched her lips with
his and kissed her solidly. Just to show her he wasn't listening to any of this "can't do this" shit.

They could damn well do anything they pleased.

When he was done, she looked at him with those big
brown eyes. "That one night isn't going to happen
again."

He raised an eyebrow and smiled.

"Really," she insisted. "It's not."

"I'm crazy about you," he said, releasing her chin and
putting the truck in gear. He'd be damned if he'd let a
woman call the shots.

"You can't be," she insisted, perfectly serious. He tried
not to smile as he drove out of town. "You're just avoiding those women your mother sent to the ranch."

"Even Carla?" he teased.

"Even Carla," Mel said, sighing. "Though I don't know why anyone would want to avoid her. She's very nice."

Ben threw the car into low gear, pulled over to the side of the empty road, stopped and took Mel in his arms. When he was done kissing her, he let her go, even though she made a little sound of protest when he released her. "There," he said, satisfied with her reaction. Mel might have a lot to say, but when he kissed her there was no mistaking the sparks between them. "I don't do *that* with Carla or anyone else. So shut up."

Mel looked around for her glasses. Somehow they'd fallen off and landed in Ben's lap. He picked them up and handed them to her. "Ever thought of wearing contacts?"

"I do. I mean, I used to," she said, putting her glasses on. "Since I've been pregnant they bother me."

"You won't be pregnant much longer," he said, looking at her abdomen. She was still tiny, but it was the middle of August already. What had she said about leaving in October?

"What are you frowning about?"

"Nothing." He moved in front of the steering wheel and pointed the truck toward home. There had to be a way to make her stay, but was he ready to be a husband? Was he ready to be a *father*?

He didn't think so, but then again, the thought of Mel packing her bags and leaving him made his blood freeze.

"HEARD CLAY'S in town."

Bonnie took a large swallow of gin before she answered. She should have known Ritter would know everything that went on in the county. "Yes."

"He's early. Why?"

She shrugged and looked away. Ritter's home was large and open, much like the Triple Bar S house. The living room smelled of good leather and the Aramis after-shave she'd given him for Christmas last year. "He won't say, but I think he's in trouble somehow. He acts like he's hiding out. And he hasn't touched a drop of whiskey."

Ritter snorted. "He's up to something, is my guess. Watch your back."

"There's no need. Clay may be a wild one, but he's not mean."

"And your son? Isn't it time you told him about us?"

Bonnie hesitated. She finished her drink, then handed the empty glass to Ritter, who took the hint and fixed her another drink. "I don't think so," she said finally, when he'd handed her a full glass. "Unless," she added, using the one weapon she knew would hit its mark, "you want to come to the barbecue and tell him yourself."

The large man shook his head, touched his glass to hers and said, "Bonnie, my love, you should have married me to start with and saved yourself a lot of trouble."

"I'm not marrying anyone. Not again."

He didn't seem to notice that she was frowning, but then again he was a calm man, a man who didn't have much to say. She'd mistaken that quiet of his for indifference thirty-five years ago and run away with a sweet-talking charmer with a knack for seduction. More's the pity.

"Your son would like a piece of King Midas," Ritter drawled. She could never think of him as Robert. His mother had always called him Ritter. He'd been the boss of the second-biggest spread in the area since he was twelve.

"It wouldn't kill you to share some of that with the Triple Bar S."

Ritter smiled and sat beside Bonnie on the couch. He put his arm around her and gave her an affectionate squeeze. "It's too much fun to see you try to get something you can't have. Marry me and I'll send that boy of yours more King Midas gold than his heifers can handle."

"No way, Ritter," Bonnie muttered, but she smiled at him. "Are we going to talk about bulls all afternoon?"

He took her in his arms. "No, but it's given me a good idea."

Bonnie went willingly and prayed that Ben hurried up and realized he shouldn't let Carla get away. If this didn't work, she'd have to figure out how to get her hands on the most sought-after bull in Texas.

So to speak.

MEL WANTED to resist him, she really did. She wanted to go into her room and shut the door and put on her baggiest nightshirt and drink a glass of iced tea and read the latest issue of *Good Housekeeping*.

But the house was dangerously empty. There was a note from Clay saying he'd taken Carla for a tour of Dallas and not to expect them back until late. Bonnie wasn't due back for days and then, Ben had promised, she'd be full of plans for the party.

"Mel," Ben said, coming into the kitchen while she was filling her glass with ice.

"Yes?" She knew, though. She'd been thinking the same thing and wishing she hadn't fallen in love with him. He was so different from John, which confused her. Maybe she hadn't been really in love with John, after all. Maybe it had been something comfortable that had grown out of working together every day. Until it had become too uncomfortable for John, that is. He'd had no intention of being around when she needed him. Mel patted her abdomen. She and her baby were going to be just fine all by themselves.

"Can I have some of that?" he said, looking at the pitcher of cold tea she'd set on the counter.

Maybe they weren't thinking the same thing after all. "Sure." He started to come over to the counter but she stopped him. "Sit down," she said. "I'll get it for you. My day off is tomorrow, not today." Even though she'd been acting like it was.

"Don't start that housekeeper bull with me, Mel." He took off his hat and set it on the table, then sprawled in a chair with his legs spread out and faced her. Mel put the glass of tea in front of him, but he spread his knees apart and took her hands, then guided her toward him. To her embarrassment he spoke to her abdomen. "Your mama is one stubborn woman, kid."

"Ben—" She tried to pull away, but he wouldn't release her hands.

"And she's always trying to get away from me, too. Which isn't fair, since I figure she should know I'm about as in love as a man can get."

"Ben," she said, looking at the top of his head. He lifted his gaze to meet hers. "Don't."

"Too late," he drawled. "It's a done deal."

"Well, undo it, because the last thing I want to talk about is love." It hurt to say the word. And the word didn't mean anything, anyway.

He gave her a level look, then brought one of her hands to his lips. "You're a hard woman, Miss Mel, but I love you anyway."

"Stop it," she whispered, hoping she wouldn't fall into his lap. She didn't want to make a fool of herself and she didn't want to set her considerable bulk onto the weight of one thigh. Even a strong man like Ben might never recover.

"No."

"It's the cinnamon rolls," she said, while he kissed each finger and nudged her closer to the juncture of his thighs. "Next time advertise for a woman who knows her way around sweet dough."

"Yes, ma'am," he agreed, but he urged her onto his lap and nibbled at her earlobe. "Anything else?"

"Make sure she doesn't mind sweeping cow manure from the porch." She did like the way his lips trailed along her neck. Mel thought about moving away and couldn't. One of his hands rested suggestively under her abdomen and made her feel a little breathless.

"Sure. I understand." The other hand started unbuttoning the front of her dress.

"Ben! What if someone comes in?"

"They'll go right back out again, I guess." He looked at her. "But you're right. I think we ought to finish this somewhere more private." With that, he scooped her into his arms and carried her upstairs to his bed.

She wished it didn't feel so right. "I weigh a ton," she protested, but he'd already negotiated the stairs, kicked the bedroom door shut behind him and sat down on the bed. She was still cradled in his arms, nestled on his lap just like they'd never left the kitchen.

"Yeah," he said, barely out of breath. "It's a good thing I'm in shape."

"You're always carrying me somewhere."

"It's the only way I can get you to go where I want."

Ben, forever practical, was right. He finished unbuttoning the top half of the dress. She wondered what he'd do if she owned dresses with back zippers. Then when he touched her breasts she forgot to think at all. They'd grown sensitive and heavy these past weeks.

She forgot to be shy. She also forgot that even with the shades drawn, there was still enough light to see how big she'd grown. But Ben didn't seem to mind. He removed her clothes with big gentle hands, then removed his own with a few swift motions, swearing softly when one of his boots didn't cooperate. Mel lay on her side, the sheet covering her, while she watched him turn to join her under the covers.

He reached for her and held her as close as her belly would allow. He kissed her until she thought she'd die of pleasure as his fingers caressed the rest of her body. When she was slick from wanting him, he threw the covers toward the foot of the bed and began to move closer. But Mel stopped him.

She rubbed her nose in the thick hair covering his chest and made him laugh. She took a flat male nipple between her lips and made his laughter stop, then took her time exploring the rest of his body.

"Mel," he groaned, but she took him in her mouth. She wanted to taste him and slide her tongue over the intriguing texture of smooth heated skin. After long minutes he lifted her off him and, breathing hard, set her on her back. He entered her slowly, though she knew he was holding back so he wouldn't hurt her. He was bigger than last time, or at least he felt that way. But she was sensitive from being touched, and her skin was electrified with every move he made inside of her.

She came quickly. Too quickly, because she'd wanted the afternoon to last. He followed her, climaxing deep inside of her. He held himself off of her, careful that no weight was put on the baby, and slowly eased away from her. Then he lay down and tucked her against him, her buttocks pressed against him so he was free to caress her breasts and kiss the back of her neck.

"Too fast," he whispered. "We have to do this more often."

"Or not at all?"

He chuckled. "Yeah. Like there's any way to keep my hands off you."

"I know," she said, thinking of how absolutely lusty she felt. "It must be the pregnancy."

His lips nibbled her neck. "And not because we're in love with each other?"

"Love? No."

Ben lifted himself up on his elbow and peered down at her. "You seem pretty sure about that."

"I thought I was in love before, and look where it got me. This is lust, Ben. Pure and simple."

"Lust," he repeated, as if considering the word and all its meaning. He ran his hand from her shoulder down to the swell of hip. "Lust?"

"Yes. I'm sure of it."

He sat up, and her heart fell. He was leaving. She closed her eyes so he wouldn't see her disappointment. She told herself that was a good thing. She should go downstairs and get dressed and defrost something for dinner. She should forget the throbbing between her legs and the way he'd fit so perfectly inside of her.

His weight shifted on the mattress and she felt his lips move against her thighs. His hands parted her legs and shifted her onto her back. "Ben?" she whispered, looking down to see his suntanned face against her very pale thigh. "What are you doing?"

Which of course was a question only an idiot would ask, she realized.

Ben moved his lips higher and touched the most sensitive spot on her entire body with the tip of his tongue. He lifted his head for the briefest second to explain. "I thought I'd find out what lust tastes like."

"SON, YOU AND I have to have a little talk."

Ben switched on the coffeepot and looked at the clock.

Barely six. "You're up early this morning." He turned toward his father, who was dressed, shaved and ready to start the day. "You going somewhere?"

"Not right away." Clay shook his head. "I thought I taught you better."

Ben straightened, leaned against the counter and crossed his arms in front of his chest. He wore yesterday's clothes and his shirt wasn't tucked in. He was barefoot and he wanted a cup of coffee more than he wanted a shower and, damn it, a man ought to be able to have some privacy in his own home at 5:56 in the goddamned morning. He waited for his father to continue.

Clay sat down in a chair and stretched out his legs. "Next time you take Mel upstairs, have the sense to close her bedroom door first."

"I don't think that's any of your business."

"It is when I come home at one in the morning and head to my room and see the housekeeper's door open and the room all dark. I know damn well she's not sleeping in there, son. And so would anyone else." Clay crossed one booted ankle over the other. "A man's gotta be more careful than that."

"You're right." He couldn't believe he'd been that stupid. Mel was still asleep upstairs. Short of carrying her down to her bed, he didn't have any choice but to leave her there and hope she'd wake up before Carla and Clay started having breakfast.

"She still sleeping?"

"Yeah. It's Mel's day off, so everyone has to cook their own eggs."

"Quit looking like you'd like to punch me," his father said, then grinned. "I could see this one comin' a mile away. Is it serious?"

Lust, he remembered. She'd said that's what it was, but she was wrong. "I'm thinking it might be."

Clay nodded. "Miss Mel's a real gem," he said. "No beauty queen, but beauty queens aren't your type." He ignored his son's frown. "She's sweet and kind, the sort of woman who won't let you down, I reckon. That coffee close to being done yet?"

"Close enough," Ben said, interrupting the brewing process to pour them both a mugful. He replaced the carafe and the coffee began to drip into it once again. Then, remembering his father liked more milk than coffee, he grabbed the milk from the refrigerator. Clay got up, fished a spoon out of the drawer and stirred milk into his coffee until it was a pale tan.

"Let's talk about your mother," Clay said.

Ben choked on his first swallow of black coffee. "Let's not."

"No, son," Clay drawled. "I think we've got to get a few things straight."

Ben's eyes narrowed. Clay was up to something and trying not to show it. "Like what?"

"Like keeping Bonnie out of our business." He took a careful sip of the coffee. "Damn, that's good."

"I've never been able to keep Bonnie out of anything she wanted to be in."

"This time's different," Clay assured him. "You're smart enough and old enough to listen to the voice of wisdom. This time you're gonna follow my directions, and everything is going to be just fine."

Ben listened, and when his father was finished, the two men shook hands. If Ben had any doubt the plan would work, he didn't voice it.

A deal was a deal.

MEL STRIPPED BEN'S BED and washed the sheets before she left for town. She didn't see Ben. She'd listened carefully at the door, wearing her rumpled sundress, before she'd crept barefoot down the stairs. The house was empty, so she supposed Ben had gone to work and maybe Carla and Clay had gone with him. Someone had mentioned something about calves the other night. She didn't want to think about Ben, and she didn't want to think that she was missing him this morning.

She showered and dressed quickly, then went into the kitchen for some toast and tea. And some eggs, she decided, feeling ravenous. Someone had made the coffee and put the breakfast dishes in the dishwasher. The counters were wiped clean, and the kitchen table held a neatly folded newspaper.

All was right with the world. Except that she had fallen in love with Ben Bradley, a wealthy rancher with a beautiful houseguest and parents who would never approve of their son's interest in the pregnant housekeeper.

She had to face it, Mel decided. She had to leave before this went too far. She was already in love with him, which was crazy. He'd mentioned love, but men liked to talk of love when they were thinking about sex. It was time to leave, before things got any more complicated. Before her heart—battered and bruised as it was—cracked completely in half. She would call Christine and tell her it was time to come to Dallas. Mel looked in her closet. How would she fit all those new maternity clothes in her suitcase?

11

MEL HUNG UP the phone and sat down in the empty kitchen. Somehow she should have known it wouldn't be easy to leave the ranch. Lately, things were just too complicated. Christine's in-laws were visiting. The tiny house would be bulging with people. If she'd told Chris the truth—that she was running away from the ranch— Chris would have said, "Come anyway," but Mel knew better. It wasn't right to add one more person—more like one and a half people—to the already crowded household.

She'd met her sister's in-laws several times. They were nice people, but they lived in Chicago and didn't get to visit often. Christine would be up to her ears in entertaining and didn't need a pregnant, weepy sister to care for, too.

"The kids are having a ball with all this attention," Chris had said. "Can you get away to come up and visit later on? We can start apartment hunting."

"Sure," she'd told her, not ready to confide that she was in love with her boss. It would sound stupid, even to her younger sister's ears. She hadn't said she was tired, ready for a change, ready to quit her job early. "That's a great idea," she'd said, so her sister wouldn't worry.

Mel thought of going to a motel, but there wasn't anything close to where her sister lived. And besides, that would use up too much of her savings.

Mel looked around the huge kitchen. She could stay here, have her baby, keep earning money and raising her child. There was room for a high chair, a playpen, a child. But she couldn't stay now, not loving Ben. He didn't seem to be a man who wanted to get married. Lord knows, he'd made that clear. And she didn't want to stay on the ranch and be a convenient sex partner. Her child deserved more than growing up knowing her mother slept with the boss.

No matter how wonderful a man the boss was.

If Ben wasn't ready to be a husband then he sure wasn't ready to be a father. Especially not to someone else's child. She was stuck here for now, but she'd leave as soon as she could. And until she did, she'd stay away from the source of her trouble.

"What's this?" Ben walked in and lifted her suitcase waist-high.

"My suitcase."

"You going somewhere?"

"I'm thinking about it." She lifted her chin and tried to stare him down.

"Back to Houston?"

"No." Never back to Houston.

"Back to him?"

"Of course not."

"Your family?"

"My parents died years ago. I thought I'd visit my sister."

"You were just going to run off? I thought after last night—"

"Ben!" She stopped him before he could say anything else. Lori was upstairs making beds and could come down any minute. She lowered her voice. "Ben, that kind of thing has got to stop."

"The only thing that's got to stop is you fighting what's between us."

"There's nothing between us," she insisted, knowing he could hear the lie in her voice.

Ben gave her a disgusted look, left the room, then returned moments later without the case and holding a brown box instead. "I put it back in your room," he said. "You shouldn't have left it in the hall. I almost broke my neck."

"What's that?"

He crossed the room and handed her the box. "You got something in the mail, honey. From Candy Corbin."

Mel tried to open it, but Ben pulled out a jackknife and slit the tape for her.

"Thanks." She separated the cardboard flaps and lifted a layer of tissue paper to reveal a tiny, child-size cowboy hat.

"What the hell is that?"

"A hat." She read the card, then lifted the hat out of the box and held it up to Ben. "Candy had the rattlesnake skin made into a hat band. She said she's sorry about shooting the 'damn varmint' and she wishes me luck."

"Nice," he said, considering the hat. "Looks pretty good."

"There's a return address. I'll have to write to her."

"You do that, sweetheart." He bent over and kissed her. Hard.

"Don't get your suitcase out again. You're not going anywhere, damn it. I've got too much work to do to go off chasing you, but I will if I have to."

With that said, he opened the slider and went outside into the bright afternoon sun.

Mel patted her abdomen. "We'll be out of this place as soon as we can," she told the baby. "The doctor said we're both doing fine." Of course, the doctor had no idea that she'd fallen in love with Ben Bradley, a man committed to staying single.

She had a knack for finding men like that.

"I COULDN'T BE HAPPIER," Bonnie gushed, kissing Ben's cheek. "I just had a feeling—"

"Bonnie," Ben interrupted. "What are you talking about?"

"Your father told me that Carla was going to stay for a while longer, maybe even until the barbecue!"

"Oh." He'd almost forgotten. "Yeah, that's right."

"Well." His mother beamed, taking his arm and leading him into the kitchen. "Fix me a drink and tell me all about it. She's a lovely girl. Is it ... intimate, yet?"

He cleared his throat as Mel looked up with wide eyes. She'd gone pale. "I'm not discussing my private life with you, Bonnie."

"Last time you were worried about your private parts. Mel, could we have some iced tea? No, never mind. I think I'll have a gin and tonic. Benjamin?"

"No. I'm going—"

"Wait," she said, releasing his arm and shoving him into a chair. "Stay right here while I get the gin." She hurried toward the bar in the living room, leaving Ben alone with Mel. She wouldn't look at him and kept peeling potatoes.

"Mel?" he said, hoping to make her look at him.

She didn't. "I'm busy," she said. "Too busy to talk about your love life."

Bonnie hurried into the room, a bottle in her hand. Mel and Ben watched as she fixed herself a tall drink and hummed "The Yellow Rose of Texas."

"Now," she said, sitting down opposite her son. "Tell me, what do you like most about her?"

Ben glanced over at Mel, who looked away. "Well," he drawled. "She laughs at my jokes."

"That's it?" Bonnie looked disappointed, so Ben continued.

"And she's real nice to everyone on the ranch," he said. "The dogs like her, too. She doesn't mind a little dirt on the floor."

"She doesn't?"

"Nope. And she knows I like my bacon burned," he said, knowing full well that Mel was listening to every word and knew he wasn't describing the latest houseguest. "She's gained a little weight since she's been here. But it looks good on her."

"I hadn't noticed," Bonnie said. "She seemed trim enough to me."

Ben tried not to laugh. "I never liked skinny women."

"Well." Bonnie breathed, sitting back in her chair and taking another swallow of her drink. "I guess I did a good job."

"We'll see," he said, hoping he hadn't gone too far. He'd made a deal with Clay, but he sure as hell hoped it wouldn't backfire on him. Bonnie could get the bit between her teeth and be hard to head off. He stood up and headed toward the door. "One thing, Bonnie." She waited, her eyes lit with excitement. "Not one word to Carla about this. She's agreed to stay on here until the barbecue. Cl—I told her it was something she shouldn't miss."

"All right." His mother lifted her glass as if making a toast. "I'll drink to that."

Ben adjusted his hat and headed outdoors. His mother had fallen for that load of bull crap, just like Clay had said she would. Bonnie Bradley believed what she wanted to believe, saw what she wanted to see. Reality didn't enter into it. Ben started to whistle. Carla, entranced with Clay's rugged charms, had happily accepted his invitation to stay until Labor Day. Ben was acting like the perfect host. Bonnie would have to come up with King Midas in time for breeding season, and Mel was staying where she belonged—right here with him.

It was turning out to be a pretty damn good day.

MEL SERVED PEAS for dinner. A great big bowl of them, steaming hot and dusted with pepper and melted butter, placed right in front of Ben where he would have to smell them.

"Peas," he said, looking at her. "Peas?"

"Your favorite," Mel said, wishing she could take a picture of the dismayed expression on his big handsome face. "Isn't it?"

"Why, no, darlin'," he said. "I think you must have me confused with someone else."

"I'll take 'em," Clay said, reaching for the bowl. "Haven't had peas in years."

They were eating in the kitchen, all five of them. Ben had demanded that she set a place for herself, and Mel was afraid he'd make a fuss if she resisted. He was acting so bossy she thought she'd take him down a peg. Luckily, Joyce had a couple of cans of peas in her pantry she was happy to let her have. *No green vegetables. Eat here, sit here, stay here.* Ben was happy to give orders.

She was happy to ignore them. At least about the green vegetables. She'd have to fix broccoli tomorrow. Or a nice spinach casserole.

"I love peas," Carla said. "Everything looks delicious, Mel."

Mel tried to smile. Just because the woman was staying for three more weeks didn't mean that Ben was going to fall in love with her. Clay was already eating out of her hand, and *he* was supposed to be the experienced lady-killer in the family. "Thank you."

"The chicken is fabulous," Bonnie added. "Wasn't this supposed to be your day off?"

"Yes, but I took some time Sunday instead, remember? I saw—"

"Oh, yes," Bonnie said, cutting her off. "Sunday."

Mel ignored Ben's wink. He was not going to charm her tonight. She was determined to resist him from now until the end of August, when she could pack her bags and flee to Dallas. She would stay until the barbecue was over. It wasn't fair to Bonnie to leave before that, and the woman had been good to her. She'd have to find another doctor, but Christine had an obstetrician, of course. She would just be escalating her plans by a few weeks, that's all. She would be settled somewhere by the time the baby arrived.

"Miss Mel?"

Mel looked up to see Clay looking at her. His expression was kind, though, as he waited for her to notice him. "I'm sorry," she said. "I guess I was daydreaming."

He smiled. "Probably thinking about your baby, am I right?"

"Well—"

"Thought of a name yet? Pass me those potatoes, darlin'. They look real good."

She lifted the bowl and handed it across the table to him, where he sat beside Ben. Carla was beside her and Bonnie at the end, positioned as queen of the house, naturally. "I haven't picked out names yet," she told him. "I don't know whether it's a boy or a girl."

"Didn't you want to know?" Carla asked.

"No. I wanted to be surprised."

"I knew Benjamin was a boy," Bonnie announced. "He had a kick like a mule."

"Mel wants a daughter," Ben told his mother.

Clay looked surprised. "That right, honey?"

"Yes." Mel took a bite of chicken. She'd basted boneless breasts in apricot jam and soy sauce. It didn't taste too bad, she decided. The chicken was moist enough.

"Are you going to keep working after the baby's born?" Carla asked.

"No. Not for at least a year. Then I may go back to teaching. That's what I did before I came here."

"Too bad you're gonna leave," Clay said, spearing a piece of chicken. "You're the best cook the Triple Bar S has ever seen."

Ben frowned. "Mel's not—"

"I'm going to miss those cinnamon rolls," his father said, giving Ben a warning look.

"Don't worry," Mel told him. "I'll leave the recipe for the next housekeeper. It's simple enough."

"It's not going to be so simple to replace you," Bonnie said. "I wish you'd reconsider and stay here. Benjamin?" She looked at her son. "Do something. Make Mel stay. You *know*—no matter what happens—we're always going to need a housekeeper. You can't expect the next Mrs. Bradley to do all the work around here."

Ben eyed his mother the same way he would a three-foot rattlesnake. "The next Mrs. Bradley can do whatever the hell she wants."

Carla raised her eyebrows and looked at Clay, who shrugged his wide shoulders and started a conversation about converting the old home place into a guest house. Bonnie was soon offering a dissenting opinion, which left Mel free to finish her dinner.

"Not eating your vegetables?" Ben pointed to the small pile of peas on her plate.

"No." She didn't like peas, either, but she wasn't going to tell him that.

"You okay?"

"I'm fine," she lied. She'd be fine only when she was away from him, when she could run and hide and pretend she didn't love him. She had the overwhelming urge to throw herself into his arms and tell him so, so she picked up her empty plate and went over to the counter to make the coffee.

In a few weeks the Bradleys would have to find another housekeeper. Mel Madison was moving on.

BONNIE PLANNED the annual barbecue with the precision of a general. She made Ben and Clay go over the guest list, gave Mel detailed directions on the menu and the catering plans, and even Carla, willing to help, was put to work on the decorations. It turned out that Perfect Carla was an expert at giving parties. Mel felt fat and the baby kicked harder and longer and during many hours of the day.

Bonnie, content that the ranch chores were going to be done properly, returned to Dallas for a few days. Mel tucked a letter stating she was leaving on September 3 in Bonnie's briefcase before she left. Ben held his monthly poker game. Perfect Carla was invited to sit in on a few hands and won six dollars and thirty cents on the first hand. Mel went to bed early, refusing all offers to learn how to play.

Ben followed her into her room. "What's going on, honey? You've been avoiding me for days."

She didn't tell him that was the only way she could keep from loving him, but when he opened his arms she went into them without a whimper.

Well, maybe a little whimper.

"I've missed you," he whispered. "I'm not sleeping real well and it's all your fault."

"I'm not sleeping, either," she said against his chest. "And it's the baby's fault."

He released her and held her at arm's length. "Get your nightgown on and get in bed, Mel. You look beat."

Ben left the room and shut the door behind him, which made her feel even sorrier for herself. She brushed her teeth, washed her face, put on her nightgown and climbed into her bed. Then she smoothed her hands over her growing abdomen and made her nightly wish for a healthy child. She was more than seven months pregnant, with about eight weeks to go.

She counted the days until Labor Day and resisted calling Christine and pouring out her troubles. She'd gotten herself into this, and she'd get herself out.

"Mel?"

She turned to see Ben tiptoe into the room. He closed the door quietly behind him and started unbuttoning his shirt. "What are you doing?"

"Making sure we both sleep tonight." He sat on the bed and took off his boots, then stripped down to his briefs and T-shirt and climbed into bed beside her. "I showered before the game," he said, as Mel scooted over to give him room.

"We can't," she protested, but allowed herself to be rolled on her side and tucked into the curve of Ben's arm. "There's all sorts of people out there."

"Shh," Ben said, and kissed her neck. "I told them I was going to bed. No one cared. Now," he said, snuggling her against him. "Good night."

Mel closed her eyes. It felt so good to be held in his arms. She hated to admit it, even to herself, but she'd missed him these past days. She was lonely, she was in love, she was miserable serving him peas and broccoli and spinach.

She was asleep.

Ben woke before dawn, dressed in last night's clothes and left Mel sleeping. He'd slept like a dead man. He'd woken up with one thing on his mind—to take advantage of the warm woman snuggled in his arms. But she'd looked so comfortable he couldn't bear to wake her.

He slept with her every night after that. Bonnie stayed in Dallas, saying it was better for Ben to have time alone with Carla. She didn't want the young woman to think she'd be an interfering mother-in-law. Everyone at the ranch breathed separate sighs of relief.

So Ben was free. In the daytime he and Mel pretended to be just friends. At night he held her in his arms and felt the baby kick against his hand. He made love to her twice, but was as content to hold her. There was extra work getting ready for the barbecue. Both were tired at the end of each day. It was enough to relax and talk and be comfortable in each other's arms. It was enough to be together, Ben realized. Mel had become a lover and a friend, and yet she was going to be someone's mother soon.

Ben didn't like thinking about that.

"I THINK it's about time we had a talk."

Ben carried his boots in one hand and poured his first cup of coffee with the other. He squinted at the clock. Five-thirty, and his old man wanted to talk. "Good morning to you, too," he said, moving over to the table. He took a cautious swallow of the coffee, then sat down and pulled on his boots. "You're up early."

"I was waiting for you," Clay said. He was dressed in work clothes. "Bonnie will be here in a couple of hours, if I'm not mistaken. The shindig is in two days, so she'll be flyin' in here giving orders like she hasn't been callin' ten times a day."

Ben leaned back in his chair and picked up his coffee cup. "I'd say we're lucky she's only been calling. If she'd been here, well, she'd have driven us all crazy by now."

Clay chuckled. "She's making those caterers pull their hair out, I'll bet."

"You wanted to talk about the party?" Ben hoped his father would get to the point. There was lots to do today, and most of it involved the ranch, not getting ready for the social event of the summer.

"Nope." Clay leaned forward. "I want to know what your intentions are, son."

"Intentions?" Ben frowned.

"About the woman you've been sleeping with every night."

"You don't miss much."

"Never have," the older man said. "Unlike some people around here."

"What's that supposed to mean?"

Clay gave him a stern look. "You serious about her?"

"I don't know."

"You'd better figure it out fast. Bonnie told me Mel's given her notice. She's leaving after the party's over."

It was like taking a fist to the gut. Ben tried to take a deep breath and couldn't. "No one told me."

"Bonnie figures you know already. She told me she'd wait on hiring someone else. She seems to figure that you might be getting married and your wife's gonna want to hire her own help."

Ben swore. Then swore again. "Mel didn't say anything."

"Maybe it's not up to her to do the talking." Clay got up and refilled his coffee, topped it off with milk and sat across from his son. "Maybe it's time for you to get married, just like your mother figures."

"And you and Bonnie are such shining examples of marriage?"

His father shrugged. "Nope. We made some mistakes, but we were too much alike, I guess. Both stubborn and hardheaded and used to having our own way all the time. It didn't help that she was the only daughter of Billy Simmons, or that I was one of the hired help."

Ben winced. "Sound familiar?"

His father shook his head. "You and Miss Mel are two different people. You're more like your grandfather, though you look like me. And Mel ain't no Bonnie Lynn Simmons, that's for sure."

"Why'd you get married, then?"

"We were full of piss and vinegar then." Ben didn't point out that they hadn't changed much in that respect and let his father continue. "We ended up fighting like wildcats, but we had some good times, too. Point is," the older man said, leaning forward, "you've got to take hold of life and go after what you want."

"You saying I don't?"

"I'm sayin' that you're happy on this ranch. So if you find a good woman who makes you happy, someone you can build a life with, then don't let her go."

"You let Bonnie go."

Clay smiled. "Not exactly. It was a mutual decision, so to speak. She never liked the ranch much after her father died, and she didn't want to be a rancher's wife, and we split the oil money and went our separate ways when you were old enough to understand."

Oh, he'd understood, all right. He'd been left with a ranch to run while his father went to Vegas and his mother lived the high life in Dallas. Now they both wanted *him* to get married and settle down. He'd been settled since the day he was eighteen, something both of

his parents had conveniently forgotten. "I could ask you
the same thing. About your intentions toward Carla."

Clay had the nerve to wink. "Carla's old enough to
take care of herself. She's one hell of a woman, I'll give
you that. Bonnie picked out a good one. She won't be
happy when she finds out the wrong Bradley has las-
soed Carla."

"Let's hope she doesn't find out before the party."

"Never thought a son of mine would be a coward,"
Clay grumbled.

"I thought we had a deal."

"That was about Carla. Now I'm talking about Mel.
She needs a husband, and that baby is gonna need a
daddy. You're sleeping with her every night and when
you think no one's looking you're staring at her with big
cow eyes."

"What's your point?" Ben stood up, ready to go to
work. He'd heard more than enough, and he didn't want
to think about Mel leaving him.

"My *point*," Clay sputtered, rising to his feet to stare
his son in the face, "is I'm trying to tell you not to be an
idiot. When you get a chance for happiness you've got
to reach out and grab on to and hold on just as long as
you can, that's my *point*. I think you should use that head
of yours for thinking. Trouble is, I might be talking to
someone more stubborn than his old man."

Ben moved away, reached for his hat and slammed it
on his head before leaving the kitchen. He'd be damned
if he was going to take advice from a man who'd had
more sex than Ritter's prize bull.

"Perfect," Bonnie said, clapping her hands in delight.
Carla and Mel, standing off to the side, shared a look of
relief. The patio surrounding the pool was decorated
with Chinese lanterns, which would be lit tonight, after

dark. Bonnie had assured them that this party would last for two days, since many of the guests would bring their own motor homes and camp in the west pasture.

Since Bonnie had arrived, every available cowhand had been taking orders, setting up tables and decorating and cleaning. They all seemed used to it, though, Mel realized. It had been going on for years, and everyone was looking forward to it.

"I think the band has arrived," Carla said, pointing to a large motor home with guitars painted on the side.

"Yes. The Texas Tornadoes, Clay's favorite. Two years ago he got them so drunk they played till dawn." She shook her head. "What a party *that* was!" She turned to Mel. "I'm glad you stayed to see this, honey. We Bradleys know how to party, and I'm sure it's something you won't forget in a hurry!"

Mel agreed. "I've never seen anyone throw a party for five hundred people, that's for sure. And I've never seen so much food." Her kitchen had been taken over yesterday by caterers. Two trucks containing Dallas Dan's barbecue equipment had arrived after lunch.

Bonnie's eyes dropped to Mel's stomach. "Are you sure you're feeling all right? You look about to burst."

"I'm fine. Really." She patted her stomach. "The baby's being quiet today. I think she's in a different position."

Carla smiled. "I envy you. How much longer?"

"Six weeks." Six weeks until the baby, two days until she left the ranch. Her life had come down to counting.

"You know you can stay here until the baby comes," the older woman said, a concerned expression in her eyes.

"Thanks, but I'll be fine."

"I have my doubts about that." Bonnie sighed and looked at the cloudless sky. "No rain, thank goodness.

They'll be arriving soon." She looked at her watch. "I'm going to get dressed. I'd suggest you two do the same. Remember, Mel, you're not to work. *Everyone* who works on the ranch gets to enjoy the party. Let the caterers do their jobs."

"Yes, ma'am," Mel teased, following Bonnie into the house. Carla was right behind her, chuckling. Carla hadn't stopped smiling all morning, come to think of it. Mel wished she felt the same way.

She managed to get through the crowd of catering people in the kitchen and went into her room to take a shower. She'd bought a new dress in town on Thursday, a crisp cotton floral with short sleeves, empire bodice and a low neck. She'd picked soft yellow this time, a color to cheer her. She needed cheering. Ben hadn't slept with her in three days. She'd barely seen him at all, but she tried to tell herself it was because Bonnie had arrived and everything changed. He would have to know that she was leaving. He'd chosen not to talk about it.

It was for the best, she decided, brushing her hair and ignoring the pain in her heart. She had to get used to life without him. She might as well start now.

BEN STOOD on the other side of the pool and watched the beautiful woman in the yellow dress talk to two of the cowhands. Mel looked as if she was having a good time. The party was in full swing, the band blasting out a loud number in front of the barn. He glanced over the hedge. At least twenty couples were dancing the two-step on the wooden dance floor Oats and Jimmy had constructed. There was food everywhere, drinks served in three locations, and the gate between the hedges was left open for people to mingle. A handful of teenagers climbed out of the pool and headed to the taco buffet for nourishment. With the sky darkening, Bonnie had instructed the waiters to light the lanterns.

Mel moved slightly to the left to whisper something to Joyce, who laughed. Joyce patted Mel's abdomen and said something that made Mel smile. She was beautiful when she smiled. She hadn't smiled at him these past days. She'd been avoiding him, he figured. And he'd let her. His father's words had stuck with him, like something he couldn't get off the bottom of his boot.

He could be a father. He could even look forward to raising Mel's baby, to having someone call him Daddy. He wanted to give Mel the moon and the stars and everything in between, as long as she wouldn't leave him. It made his blood boil just to think about it.

Damn, he wanted to haul her to a quiet place and tell her she couldn't leave him. Instead he watched her. And wanted her. And tried to get close to her. But every time he got close, somebody stopped him to say hello and thank him for the party. It took him close to an hour to get around to the other side of the pool, where Mel stood sipping iced tea and looking like a buttercup.

Lord, he'd missed her.

"Mel," he tried, moving closer.

She turned to face him. "What?"

"Why didn't you tell me you were leaving soon?" He sounded harsher than he'd planned to, and a look of pain crossed her face.

"I figured you'd find out sooner or later."

"When?" he asked, stepping aside for a waiter carrying a tray of appetizers.

"Sir?" the man said, dropping the tray to serving level. "Would you care for anything?"

"Go away," Ben growled, and the waiter shrugged and moved on. Ben looked at Mel. "Didn't you think I'd notice?"

"I thought you'd notice," she answered. "Eventually. I thought it was best, before the baby came and all."

He touched her cheek. "There's something we need to talk about," he said, keeping his voice low.

"What?"

Ben raised his voice over the band's latest song. "I said, we need to talk!"

Mel winced, and he dropped his hand. "I don't think now is such a good idea."

"Mel," he began, taking a deep breath before he said what he had to say.

"Hi, guys!" Lori said, coming up behind him. She held Jack Ritter's hand and she was smiling from ear to ear. "Great party, Ben!"

"Yeah." He wanted to tell her to get lost, but he couldn't hurt her feelings. Jack looked uncertain, as if he wasn't sure he was welcome.

"Tell Jack no one's going to throw him out," Lori said. "He's trying to avoid your father."

Ben shook Jack's hand. "Glad to have you here, Jack. Maybe one of these days you can talk your old man into coming."

Jack laughed and shook his head. "Not likely, Mr. Bradley. I heard your mother trying to talk him into it last night. He wouldn't budge."

He might have asked where his mother saw Ritter last night, but his mind was on getting Mel off by herself where he could talk. Where he could beg, was more like it. He took her hand and started to lead her away. "You'll have to excuse—"

"Ladies and gentlemen," Clay's voice boomed over the loudspeaker. "Would you all gather over here by the band? I've got one hell of an important announcement to make!"

"Mel," Ben said. "Let's get out of here."

"Ben," Clay hollered, his voice even louder. "I need you up here, son!"

"Damn it," Ben grumbled, keeping hold of Mel's hand. He didn't intend to let her go. Lord knows how he could find her in the crowd if he lost her now. Lori and Jack followed them over to the bandstand, then Clay waved at Ben to join him on stage.

"Stay right there," he told Mel. "I'll be right back."

"What's going on?" she asked.

He shrugged. "Clay's had too much tequila already, I guess. He's probably going to announce his divorce again." He jumped on the stage and stood beside his father as the crowd assembled. He would give Clay ten minutes, then he was going back to his woman. *His woman.* He liked the sound of that.

"THIS IS WILD," Jack said, grinning at the women. "I'm really glad I got to come here this year."

"I know," Lori said, beaming at him. She hooked her arm through his. "Me, too. Daddy's getting better about seeing a Ritter around, don't you think?"

"Yeah, and you'll be seeing a lot more of me, too, if Ms. Bonnie marries my dad."

Lori and Mel stared at the tall young man. "What?" they asked in unison. Mel tried not to laugh at the sheepish look on Jack's face.

"Does your father have a big gold longhorn belt buckle?" she asked.

"Yeah."

"I've met him." She turned to Lori. "Bonnie went to the movies with him a few weeks ago."

"Wow," the young girl said. "Wait till I tell Mom."

"They've been together a long time," Jack said. "At least that's what my father said, and if Ben wins the bull, then Bonnie will have to marry Dad to get it. My father's been prancing around like a young bull at breedin' time." His gaze dropped to Mel's abdomen and he turned red. "Pardon me."

Mel stared at him. "If Ben wins the bull? What does that mean?" These Texas ranchers were a strange breed.

"I heard my dad tellin' my older brother about it. Ms. Bonnie made a deal with Ben. She bet she could find him the perfect woman from some magazine." He looked sorry he couldn't explain. "I don't get that part."

Mel did. "Go on anyway."

"*Please*," Lori said, tugging on her boyfriend's arm. She glanced toward the stage where Clay still held the microphone. "Hurry up before they start talking."

"The way it goes is like this. If Ms. Bonnie *can't* find a woman for Ben, then he gets King Midas. But the only way Ms. Bonnie is ever going to get that bull is if she marries Dad. He said he'd give it to her as a wedding present."

"And if Bonnie *does* find the so-called perfect woman, what does she win?"

"I think Ben has to get married."

"Married," Mel repeated, rubbing the small of her back against the ache there. "And if he doesn't, he wins a bull. Do I have this right?"

"Yep. I think my dad's been trying to get Ms. Bonnie to marry him for a long time. He said one time she was harder to rope than a three-headed steer."

Mel tried again. "Let me see if I have this right. Ben stays single and gets some important bull—"

"King Midas is one of Texas's champions," Jack inserted, pride in his voice. "I'm hopin' Ben gets married. Otherwise I lose the bull *and* get Ms. Bonnie for a stepmother." He pretended to shiver.

"But if Ben gets married, he gets the woman instead?"

"Yep."

"Mom's gonna love this," Lori said, trying to look through the crowd.

Mel looked at the stage to where Clay and Ben stood. Two identical figures, she thought. Both smiling, listening to the bass guitarist telling them something. They almost looked as if they were going to do a song.

A bull. This whole summer was over a bull. He'd used her to avoid those other women and win a bet. He'd stayed in her bed instead of someone else's so he wouldn't be tempted.

Mel stared at him. He was going to win a bull, and she was hemmed in by the crowd and couldn't walk out. In fact, she was about four weeks late in walking out on the whole crazy bunch of them.

12

BEN WATCHED HIS MOTHER and Carla move through the crowd to stand next to Mel in the front row. Mel was looking a little tired, and she rubbed her back again. The party had been too much for her. He would take her to the house and put her to bed, and maybe he'd stay there a while himself. He turned to his father. "You want to get on with whatever it is you're doing?"

"I'm just gettin' warmed up," Clay said, putting his glass on an amplifier. He grinned and turned to the crowd. "I've got somethin' to say. You all know what we celebrate here every year, the Bradley *dee*-vorce." His exaggerated accent caused a ripple of laughter through the crowd, and Bonnie lifted her glass in a silent toast. Carla smiled, and Mel stared at her. She had gone very pale. Ben resigned himself to a few more minutes of listening to his father embarrass himself, but he wasn't going to give him much more than that.

"Now," Clay continued, "we're going to celebrate a wedding." He paused as the crowd simmered down to listen. Ben stared.

"A what?"

Clay clapped his arm around Ben's shoulders. "We're going to celebrate the fact that the future Mrs. Bradley said yes today!" Ben looked out in the crowd to see who his father was beaming at. Bonnie clapped her hands along with the rest of the crowd, Carla blushed, and Mel stood there as if she was frozen to the dance floor.

Not me, he mouthed to her, but she didn't look like she understood. She spoke to Lori, who tugged at Bonnie's arm. Clay tried to shake Ben's hand, but he pulled away and jumped off the stage. "Not me," he hollered, brushing past Carla. "I'm not getting married."

One of the men standing behind Mel said, "Looks pretty clear that it's time you did, Ben." Others laughed.

"Mel?" He took her arm.

She spoke to Joyce, who had appeared behind her. "My water broke. I've been having pains for a while but I thought I was just tired."

Ben made a move to take her in his arms. "I'll carry you to—"

"Get away from me," she said, sounding aggravated with him. "I can walk."

"Like hell you will."

"I mean it, Ben." She hit him on the arm. "Go away. Someone else can give me a ride to the hospital."

He swept her into his arms anyway. "I dare them to try," he muttered, heading for the house. Over the loud-speaker he heard Clay's voice ring out.

"Well, folks, how about that? First we're having a wedding and now we're having a baby! One hell of a party, ain't it?"

The crowd cheered.

"GET OUT," Mel said when Ben walked into her hospital room. She was having labor pains every three minutes. "I don't need a cowboy to hold my hand."

"A rancher," he corrected. He sat down in the only chair and ran his hand through his hair while the nurse gave him a strange look.

"Our little mother mustn't be disturbed," the gray-haired woman said, handing Mel a cup of ice. "You can suck on that, sweetheart, if you get thirsty." She gave Ben a severe look. "You're not the husband, are you?"

"No, but—"

"Then you do as the little mother says." She made a shooing motion with her hand. "Out you go."

Ben stood. "Mel—"

"Wait," she gasped, and was silent as she breathed in and out. The nurse looked at her watch.

"They're coming closer together, honey. Right on schedule."

Ben clenched his fists and wished he could punch something. He hated to see Mel in such pain. When the contraction was over, she leaned back on the pillow and turned to him. "Will you call my sister?"

"What's her name?"

"Christine Ripley. In Dallas." She panted out a number and he memorized it.

"I'll be right back," he said, repeating the number to himself.

"Tell her the contractions are three minutes apart." Mel looked at the nurse after Ben hurried from the room. "How much longer does this go on?"

"That's up to the baby, honey. Some go quick, some don't. You're doing just fine. Want a nice cloth for your head?"

Mel shook her head. "The baby's six weeks early. This isn't supposed to be happening."

"The doctor will be here soon. He was at some big party out of town, at some ranch, but we got hold of him." The nurse started to leave the room.

"Push that button if you need me."

"Thanks."

She didn't want to be alone during the contractions, but she didn't want to admit it. So Dr. Connelly had been out at the Triple Bar S, doing the two-step with his wife and maybe even drinking tequila. Wonderful. She could have stayed on the ranch and saved everyone a trip to town. The bull-bettor himself could have continued to party instead of taking her in Bonnie's luxurious Cadillac. He'd taken the road to Rose River at ninety miles an hour and he'd never stopped swearing.

Bonnie had sat with her in the back seat and told her she'd be fine. Of course the woman would feel that way—she had a half-empty bottle of Jack Daniels tucked between her legs, a plastic glass in her hand and was well on her way to being plastered.

Mel almost laughed remembering, then the next contraction started. She lifted herself up on her elbows and tried to remember how to breathe.

"I left a message on the answering machine," Ben said, stepping into the room just as Mel leaned back on her pillows. "I told her to come to the Rose River hospital."

"Thanks. Now get out."

"What the hell is going on?" He put his hands on his hips and stood at the foot of the bed.

"I'm a little busy here," she said, looking at the clock. "I'm having a baby."

"It's Clay's announcement, isn't it? Damn," he groaned. His father's damned performance had made Mel think he was hooked up with Carla after all. "You think I'm getting married. Hell, Mel, honey, I'm not marrying Carla. Dad is."

The nurse poked her head in the door. "Doctor's on his way in." She gave Ben an evil look, which made him back up a step. "You're still here?"

"Yes, ma'am." He gulped. "I sure as hell wouldn't be anywhere else."

"Don't upset the little mother," she warned. "You can give her some ice if she wants, and keep her breathing during the contractions." She shut the door and left them alone again.

"I'm not getting married," he insisted. "Clay was talking about getting married to Carla. That's the Mrs. Bradley he was talking about."

"I know that," she said, glaring at him. "They've been making eyes at each other since they met."

"My dad makes eyes at every woman he meets."

"Not like this, I'll bet. Carla was crazy about him right off."

"She was?"

Mel looked at the clock again and got up on her elbows.

Ben moved to her side, forgetting he even had a father and that his father was getting married again. "It's starting again?"

She nodded, biting her lip.

"Breathe," he said, remembering the nurse's words.

Mel breathed. And counted while she was doing it, too, though he didn't know why. "Now leave. Go back to your bull-betting mother and celebrate your victory."

"What are you talking about?"

She looked at him, and he wondered if she was going to cry. "I spent all summer feeling sorry for you and then Jack Ritter says you were just trying to win a champion bull. Is that true?"

"Well . . ." He stalled, wondering how he could put it a little better.

"It's true then," she said, looking away. "You used the pregnant housekeeper as a diversion and—"

"Hell, honey, I never—"

"Yes, you did." She wouldn't look at him, so he went around to the other side of the bed. "You let me fall in love with you so you wouldn't be tempted by those other women."

"Tempted? By Tessie Mae or Candy?"

"By Carla, then," Mel declared. "Carla was perfect."

"Not for me. For Clay."

"Luck," she said. "That was pure luck."

"Yes," Ben agreed. "It sure as hell was. The old man's happy. And my mother will just have to accept that her plan didn't work."

"And you end up with the prize."

He looked into her sweet face and nodded. "Yes, ma'am, I sure did."

"Go to your bull then. I don't—"

The door opened and Mel stopped talking to see who was coming into the room. A young doctor in a bright red Western shirt walked over to the bed. He waited politely for the contraction to be finished before speaking to Mel. "I see you're going to have this baby before football season."

Mel looked at him with a worried expression. "Too early?"

Ben's stomach knotted. He hadn't thought about the baby being early and in danger.

The doctor shook his head. "Six weeks is all right," he said. "Though we prefer our babies stay longer."

"I must have done something wrong," Mel said.

"Any falls? Accidents? Anything like that?"

"No. I've just been more tired lately, and my back ached."

"Maybe this one just wanted to be born ahead of schedule." He smiled to reassure them, then listened to the baby's heart with his stethoscope. "Sounds strong." He turned to Ben. "Are you the birthing coach?"

"No," Mel said.

"Yes," Ben said louder. He stuck out his hand. "Ben Bradley."

"I know." The doctor shook his hand. "Mark Connelly. I was just out at the barbecue. My wife's folks are old friends of your—"

"He's not my birthing coach or anything else." Mel panted, rising up again. "Send him home."

"Mel," Ben said.

"You're no better than that damn bull," she said. "Rutting with anything placed in front of you."

Dr. Connelly grinned at Ben. "They can get real cranky during this stage of the birthing process. I'm going to ask you to leave for a second, while I check to see how dilated she is, then we'll get her hooked up to a fetal monitor. Just as a precaution." He patted her arm, and Mel started to breathe faster again.

Ben didn't want to leave, but it looked like the doc expected him to. He waited outside, but avoided the waiting room. Bonnie would be there drinking, and he had a feeling there'd be others showing up to see how Mel was doing. He'd wait until he had news. The doctor came out and took him a few steps down the hall.

"She's almost there. I've called a pediatrician and we're getting set up for a preemie. The baby will be incubated and we'll go from there."

"Is Mel in danger?"

"No. And the baby probably isn't, either, but we'd rather play it safe."

Ben nodded. "What can I do?"

"Keep her calm."

Yeah, Ben thought, watching the doctor walk to the desk to confer with a couple of nurses. *Easy for him to say*. The woman he loved thought she meant less to him than a champion bull. There was going to be a lot to straighten out after this baby was born. In the meantime, keeping calm about having a baby was going to be the hardest damn thing he'd ever done.

MEL DIDN'T WANT to hold his hand. She didn't want to need him at all, but she couldn't help it. She hung on to Ben's big fingers and listened to his voice telling her everything was going to be all right and she wanted to believe him. She really did.

She panted when they told her to pant. She pushed when someone said push. Ben moved behind her and propped her up so she could push even harder than she ever thought was humanly possible.

The baby was going to be six weeks early. That wasn't good, no matter how much Dr. Connelly tried to downplay the danger. Babies were supposed to have those extra six weeks to get fat and strong. They weren't supposed to shoot out into the world early.

Though maybe *shoot out* wasn't the best phrase, she thought, considering what hard work having a baby was turning out to be.

"Hang in there, honey," Ben said. "We're almost done."

"We?" She panted. "Since when did you start trying to push a bowling ball out of your body?"

One of the nurses gave him a sympathetic smile.

"I've got the head," the doctor announced. "Stop pushing, Mel!"

"Okay." She tried not to push, but she really wanted to.

"Now," the doctor called. "Go ahead."

She gave it her strongest effort and felt the baby slipping out of her. It was the strangest feeling, and then Ben lifted her so she could see. The doctor held a squirming bundle of red skin, and then a small cry came from the child.

"It's a girl," the doctor said, handing the baby to the nurse waiting with a blanket. "She looks healthy. Her color's good. She's just small."

"She'll grow," Ben said in her ear.

"A girl," Mel said, brushing away the tears from her cheeks. She didn't want to be blinded with tears when she wanted to see her child. The doctor cut the umbilical cord while the nurse put the infant in Mel's arms.

"Meet your mama," the woman said, smiling.

The baby's face was scrunched and crying, but Mel thought she'd never seen anything more beautiful in her whole life. Her little arms flailed, her ten little perfect fingers clenched tight. "She's so beautiful."

"Like her mother," Ben whispered, still holding Mel in his arms. "Look, she has your nose."

"She does?" Mel thought she looked a little like her mother, but she wasn't sure. All that mattered was that she was alive and healthy. The nurse took her back.

"We've got to clean up this little lady," she said. "She'll be in the incubator for the next twenty-four hours, just to make sure everything stays fine."

"Do you have to take her away?"

The nurse bundled the baby in her arms. "You rest up," she said. "Does this little sweetheart have a name?"

"Not yet."

"Well, you think of a name for this baby while we do our work, all right?"

Mel nodded. She was hungry and excited and felt like she could sleep for a week. "Okay."

The nurse paused by Ben. "Does Daddy want to hold his daughter?"

"He's not—"

"Yes," Ben said, clearing his throat. "Daddy does." Mel turned as Ben moved off the bed and let the nurse place the baby in his arms. She looked ridiculously small in the rancher's big arms, and Ben looked terrified. It was hard to stay mad at him when he was holding her daughter. The nurse carefully lifted the baby out of Ben's arms.

"Come on, sweetheart," she said. "Let's get you cleaned up."

Ben looked up when Mel looked at him, then she turned away and closed her eyes. She was finished here. Finished with Rose River and the Triple Bar S and a rancher named Ben. A whole new life had begun in more ways than one.

HE STAYED WITH HER while the doctor finished up. He shook hands with Connelly and told him he would be sending a side of beef to his house first thing Monday morning. Then Ben walked beside Mel when they moved her to her room, sat in the chair and watched her until her eyes closed and her breathing grew even. Ben didn't move until he was certain Mel wouldn't need him for a while, then he slipped out of the room and found his way to the small waiting area.

"It's a girl," he announced right away. The place was so crowded that some of the ranch hands had to stand. Bonnie stood up and wobbled over to him.

"What about Mel?"

"She's fine." He grasped his mother's arm and helped her to her seat. An empty whiskey bottle sat by her foot. "The baby's small but the doctor said she should be fine once she puts on a little more weight."

They cheered. Clay clapped his son on the back, Carla hugged him and Lori cried. The young Ritter kid grinned from ear to ear, while Jimmy and Joyce hugged each other, then came toward Ben.

"A little girl," Joyce said. "How wonderful for Mel. She wanted a daughter." Jimmy looked like he was going to cry.

"Can we see the baby?" Oats asked, fanning himself with his hat.

"Not till tomorrow." He turned to his father. "You all go back to the party and celebrate. Mel should be sleeping for a while. She's pretty tired."

"All right," his father agreed, slapping him on the back one more time. "Remember what I said to you, now."

"Take hold of life?"

He winked. "Yep. Grab it and hold on." He turned to the rest of the people in the waiting room. "Let's go back to the ranch and drink a toast to a new little Texan."

Ben left the room while they were congratulating each other. There was still something left to do before he felt like celebrating anything.

THE FIRST THING she noticed when she woke up was the darkness outside the hospital window. She blinked, wondering how long she'd slept.

"Three hours," Ben said, reading her mind. She turned toward the sound of his voice in the dimly lit room. "It's the next day already."

"Is everything okay with the baby?"

"I was just down in the nursery. She's asleep and doing fine. They said if all goes as planned they'll bring her to you tomorrow. And you can visit her anytime you want."

She made a move to sit up and Ben shoved pillows behind her head. "Why are you still here?"

"I didn't want you to be alone."

"I don't mind," she lied.

"And I thought we'd better get something straight, before that little girl gets any older."

"Go home to your new bull, Ben," she said, hoping he wouldn't listen to her. She wished he'd hold her again. She wished he'd tell her he loved her, so she could tell him he was crazy and then she could believe him, deep down in her heart.

"Shut up about the bull. You're just trying to use that as an excuse to kick me out." He smiled and moved his chair closer to the bed. He stroked her hair from her forehead. "I want to talk about our daughter. You're going to marry me, aren't you?"

"You don't have to marry me, Ben. Just because you saw her born doesn't mean—"

"I don't have to do anything," he muttered. "I was trying to ask you before, at the barbecue. I was trying to get you to stay."

Mel felt him take her hand. "Your mother wanted you to find the perfect woman. Not a pregnant house-keeper."

"My mother's not in love with you," he said softly. "I am."

"You're just caught up in the excitement of the baby being born."

He smiled, that familiar smile that made his dark eyes twinkle. "Sweetheart, I'm a man in love. I've been trying to tell you that for weeks."

"You have?"

"Admit it, Mel," he said. "You need me around. You like to pretend you don't need anyone, but you need me." He placed a gentle kiss on her knuckles. "Don't you?"

She hesitated, unwilling to admit that he was right. He'd been there for her all along, only she was trying not to see it. She hadn't wanted to get hurt again. She hadn't wanted to depend on anyone ever again.

"I guess I do," she said softly. "How'd you get so smart?"

"I eat my vegetables."

She laughed until his lips touched hers. He kissed her for a long, wonderful moment and then sat back on the chair. "One of these years I'd like a son, too."

A son. She'd like that. "You think I'm going through this again?" Mel teased.

He chuckled. "Tell you the truth, I'm not sure my heart could take it. I've never been so scared in my life."

"You were very brave."

"I wouldn't expect you to marry a coward."

Mel smiled at him. "That's okay, Ben. Nobody's perfect."

Epilogue

"THAT CHILD needs a name," Bonnie declared. She took the cup of coffee Ben handed her and sat in a plastic chair. The waiting room was empty now, so she crossed her legs and raised her voice a little.

"Rose," Ben said. "Mel's decided her name is Rose."

Bonnie nodded, satisfied. She sipped her coffee. "Do you have any aspirin on you?"

"No." Ben sat in a chair across from his mother. "You could ask a nurse."

"They're still mad about the whiskey."

"I don't think you're supposed to bring your own bottle into the hospital." He leaned back and closed his eyes. Mel's sister had finally arrived, and the two of them were in the room talking about babies and weddings. "Why are you still here?"

"To give you a ride home, of course."

"I'll drive," he said quickly, remembering the empty bottle he'd tossed in the wastebasket.

"Fine. Whatever." She paused. "We've got to keep her, Benjamin. You can't let the best cook we've ever had just walk away."

Ben opened his eyes and studied his mother. Every silver-blond hair was in place, her ruffled skirt was immaculate, her silver bracelets gleaming. Even the ruby lipstick was applied with perfection. "Don't you have any idea what's gone on here today?"

Bonnie sniffed. "Of course I do. Your father is marrying Carla. Stole her right from under your nose, the horny old cowhand did. He's even buying a ranch west of town. We'll be neighbors." Her eyes narrowed. "And *you* let it happen."

He couldn't resist teasing her just a little. "And you owe me one champion bull. You didn't find the perfect woman for me from that magazine, did you?"

She lifted her gaze to his face and looked as if she was going to cry. "Oh, Benjamin, don't make me. The only way I can get that bull is to marry Ritter."

Ben couldn't help laughing. "What happened? I thought there was a feud."

"Between Ritter and Clay. It happened a long time ago. When I ran off with Clay. I didn't know Ritter was in love with me, you see. He never *said* anything, so I'd given up on him. I came back married to Clay and he swore he'd never set foot on anything with the Bradley name on it again."

"Except after the divorce."

She surprised him by blushing. "Ritter and I have an . . . arrangement, Benjamin. But I sure don't want to get married. And he won't give me the bull unless I do." She gave her son a pleading look. "Let me buy you another bull. A *better* bull. Please, Ben?"

"I'll think about it. I kinda had my heart set on old Midas, though." Ben put his hands behind his head and considered letting her off the hook. "By the way, I'm hiring a new housekeeper," he said.

"You can't talk Mel into staying?"

"Oh, I've done that already," he said. "She's going to marry me."

Bonnie opened her mouth but nothing came out. Ben thought she looked like a very expensive fish gasping for air. He waited, because he knew his mother would have something to say eventually.

"Married," she said in a low voice. "Married?"

He nodded. "I'll be a husband and a father, all at once."

"She'll make you a wonderful wife," she declared, then smiled, a satisfied smile that looked almost frightening. "I won after all," she declared.

"No, you didn't."

Triumph was written all over her face. "I found Mel. I was the one who hired her. That was the bet, remember? That I could find you the perfect woman. Now," she declared, leaning back in her chair. "You owe me a wedding."

"I owe you more than a wedding." Accident or not, his mother had brought Mel to him, and his life would never be the same again.

"A wedding will be enough," she declared, humming the bridal march under her breath. "Mel's sister will be matron of honor. And I will hold Rose, of course, while you take your vows."

"Of course."

"And we'll have the reception at the ranch."

"If Mel agrees," Ben cautioned.

"I'll take care of it," Bonnie said, standing up and brushing imaginary wrinkles from her skirt. "Now, take me to see my granddaughter. I hear she's a pretty little thing."

"Yes, she is," Ben said, taking his mother's arm. Bonnie paused to discreetly wipe her eyes while he pretended not to notice. "She's downright beautiful."

HARLEQUIN®

Temptation

MEN OF WHISKEY RIVER

Three sexy, unforgettable men
Three beautiful and *unusual* women

Come to Whiskey River, Arizona, a place "where anything can happen. And often does," says bestselling author JoAnn Ross of her new Temptation miniseries. "I envision Whiskey River as a romantic, magical place. A town like Brigadoon, hidden in the mists, just waiting to be discovered."

Enjoy three very *magical* romances.

#605 *Untamed* (Oct.)

#609 *Wanted!* (Nov.)

#613 *Ambushed* (Dec.)

Come and be spellbound

Look us up on-line at: http://www.romance.net

MOWR-G

Merry Christmas, Baby!

A romantic collection filled with the magic
of Christmas and the joy of children.

SUSAN WIGGS, Karen Young and
Bobby Hutchinson bring you Christmas wishes,
weddings and romance, in a charming
trio of stories that will warm up your
holiday season.

MERRY CHRISTMAS, BABY! also contains
Harlequin's special gift to you—a set of
FREE GIFT TAGS included in every book.

Brighten up your holiday season with
MERRY CHRISTMAS, BABY!

Available in November at
your favorite retail store.

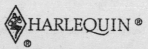

HARLEQUIN ®

Look us up on-line at: http://www.romance.net   MCB

REBECCA

43 LIGHT STREET

YORK

FACE TO FACE

*Bestselling author Rebecca York returns to "43 Light Street"
for an original story of past secrets, deadly deceptions—and
the most intimate betrayal.*

She woke in a hospital—with amnesia…and with child.
According to her rescuer, whose striking face is the last
image she remembers, she's Justine Hollingsworth. But
nothing about her life seems to fit, except for the baby
inside her and Mike Lancer's arms around her. Consumed
by forbidden passion and racked by nameless fear, she
must discover if she is Justine…or the victim of some mind
game. Her life—and her unborn child's—depends on it….

Don't miss *Face To Face*—Available in October, wherever
Harlequin books are sold.

HARLEQUIN ®

®

43FTF

Look us up on-line at: http://www.romance.net

Mail Order Men—Satisfaction Guaranteed!

Texas Man 3—*Travis Holt*

Running a ranch and raising three nieces is a real handful for this ex-rodeo champ, and he needs a good woman—fast.

Eve Reardon is willing to gamble on Travis if it means a secure home for her infant son. Love isn't part of the deal, but when their marriage of convenience becomes a passionate affair, Eve's heart is at stake. And Travis risks everything to win a nearly impossible prize: her trust.

#608 LUCK OF THE DRAW
by Candace Schuler

Available in October wherever
Harlequin books are sold.

HARLEQUIN *Temptation*

Look us up on-line at: http://www.romance.net

MMEN2

When all the evidence points to love,
there's only one verdict.

VERDICT:
Matrimony

Witness the power of love this September as
seasoned courtroom lawyers discover that
sometimes there's just no defense against love.

This special collection of three complete stories
by your favorite authors makes a compelling
case for love.

WITHOUT PRECEDENT by JoAnn Ross
VOICES IN THE WIND by Sandra Canfield
A LEGAL AFFAIR by Bobby Hutchinson

Available this September wherever Harlequin
and Silhouette books are sold.

HARLEQUIN ®
®

Silhouette®
™

Look us up on-line at: http://www.romance.net

HREQ996